MW01140256

Dogs and More Dogs, Another Murder

A Sheridan Hendley Mystery

CHRISTA NARDI

Cover Design by Victorine Lieske

CHAPTER 1

The holiday decorations were packed away, the house no longer festive. I'd procrastinated much longer than any other year and now even New Year's was a memory. Married to State Police Detective Brett McMann and stepmom to his teenaged daughter, Maddie, about six months now.

I was sad to put our first Christmas as a family behind us. Still, I was truly relieved the hustle and bustle was over. Juggling two families had been stressful, though time with my parents and sibs, Kaylie and Kevin, was good. Drinking my never empty coffee, I relished the quiet and uncluttered living area.

"Sheridan, can I go skating with Nedra and Willie? Miss Melina is taking us."

"Is your room clean? And what time will you be home?" Melina and I both volunteered at the local dog shelter, and her daughter, Nedra, was in Maddie's eighth grade class. Little did Maddie know, Melina had texted me already about taking them skating. She

1

knew I was volunteering at Pets and Paws today and this would give Maddie something to do. Winter break is great for a few days and then it gets old.

"Yes, my room is clean. I'll be home before dinner."

"Okay. Let's make sure you have everything and you're ready when they get here to pick you up."

I followed her to her room, our two dogs, Charlie and Bella padding behind us. Sometimes Maddie's teen version of a clean room and mine didn't quite look the same. At least on the surface, this time we were on the same page. Even Bella's toys were all assembled in her bed.

"Heavy socks, so you don't get blisters? Extra layers or a coat? It can get cold out there with the wind." The weather had been pretty mild for Virginia in January so far, with only a few nights of frost, and mostly in the 40s.

The eighth grader made a face. "Jeesh, I'm not a child. Besides extra layers make me look fat."

"But you'll be warm. What about the thermals? They're thin and help retain heat and then you might get by without a jacket."

"Okay. Okay. Can you get my skates?"

"On it. Skates, gloves, scarf and hat coming up." I ignored her eye roll and gathered everything together as Melina pulled up.

"Hurry up. They're here." She bustled out of the room, grabbed everything and was out the door. I waved to Melina from the door.

Only a few more days and Maddie would be back at school and I'd be back to work at Millicent College teaching on Wednesdays and Fridays. I finished my coffee and cleaned up. After letting Charlie and Bella out, I headed for Pets and Paws.

Smiling, I remembered the way Mrs. Chantilly had all the dogs decked out in bells, bows, and bowties before Christmas. Pets and Paws was in an old colonial home. Mrs. Chantilly lived upstairs and the dogs were downstairs. With Luke's help, she'd decorated the house, inside and out. She'd always reminded me of Mrs. Claus and for two weeks she dressed the part and bounced around with abundant enthusiasm. More than one of the dogs managed to destroy her holiday trappings around the place from time to time, but she took it in stride.

The house was on the news and people came from all over to view it. She'd go out and invite them in to see the rest of the decorations – and the dogs. Not unintentionally, by any means, she managed to get many dogs adopted.

I chuckled to myself, recalling when she'd tried singing traditional holiday songs. Unlike me, she had a beautiful voice. The problem was with some of the dogs. They tried to sing, only the howling was not quite in tune. Sure enough, as I pulled up in front of the house I noticed the decorations were gone from Pets and Paws now, too.

Luke was moving boxes and grunted hello as I arrived. A high school student with some bad habits, like the stray and rescue dogs Mrs. Chantilly collected, Luke was a restoration project. His legal issues led to his "volunteering" at Pets and Paws. When he first started his community service there, he scowled a lot and made me nervous. He was still an entitled beachboy type.

He'd made some attitude adjustments in the past few months and I was glad to see it. I still didn't quite trust him despite Mrs. Chantilly always singing his praises. She met me at the door, grandmotherly, only without the Mrs. Claus attire. I also noted the bounce in her step was gone. Even though she had to be in her sixties, she always seemed to have energy and a happy face.

"Isn't this weather just delightful? Sunny, not too, too cold. I heard it's going to freeze tonight and maybe snow. Those abandoned dogs wouldn't survive if that happened."

Now used to her manner of speech, I simply asked, "What abandoned dogs?"

"Over at the Stoneham place of course, near Blake Buchanan's. Have you ever been to his home? It is beautiful. A mansion fit for a king. His wife, Ava, studied interior decorating you know."

"No, I didn't know. Did they find dogs at the Stoneham's?"

"That's what I said. Nobody ever bothered the Stonehams for many years. Older couple and all, their children grown and gone, they kept to themselves. Justine and Herman didn't live there when I was growing up here. Someone else did though. Never knew who they were."

Mrs. Dora Chantilly had left Clover Hill after high school and she'd only returned when her grandmother died and left her the house, now Clover Hill Pets and Paws. Her grandmother had taken in strays and the place was a mess. I was about to ask again about the dogs, and an SUV pulled up.

"Here they are with more of the dogs. Poor things. Luke and I already fed and bathed the first group Blake brought over. I'm sure glad you're here to help."

I followed her as she hurried to the car and greeted Blake Buchanan, former mayor of Clover Hill. He took her in his arms and then seemed to realize I was there. He and Mrs. Chantilly had been an item in high school and they renewed their friendship when she returned.

"Dora, we uncovered a mama and pups." He shook his head. "One of them didn't make it. Dane mix. Where's Luke? Even malnourished, it'll take two of us to get her and her pups inside." Mrs. Chantilly rushed to open the door and see to the animals.

"Mr. Buchanan, can you fill me in? Mrs. Chantilly hasn't had a chance yet."

He smiled and his eyes twinkled. We both understood that sometimes she was a bit hard to follow. Almost like putting a puzzle together. Me, I prefer things to be in order when someone is telling me a story.

"Last night, I was sitting on the deck and my dog, Bridgit, showed up with a puppy, not in good shape. As soon as I took the pup, she darted in the direction of the Stoneham place. I called to my wife, put the pup in a blanket, and took off after her."

He paused for effect.

"The house was dark but Bridgit stood at the front porch and dug to get further underneath. I knocked at the door and no one answered. I called Chief Peabody. Aiming my flashlight under the porch, I got a look at dogs huddled together. With help, we extracted six dogs and two more puppies and brought them here."

He shuddered. "Such bad shape. Bridgit still wasn't happy, but that was all we could do last night. Four of us have been on the property this morning. Brought four more dogs earlier. Butch and Bridgit, my best dogs, are helping us wade through it."

"Huh? What do you mean 'wade through it' – is the house that much of a mess?"

"That's a mild description. Stuff stacked on top of stuff on top of stuff, and the smell." He shuddered again. "This mama and her pups were in the kitchen. We could hear yelping from other parts of the house."

"Here comes Luke. We need to get these dogs inside. Sheridan, can you start some formula going? These pups are near starved to death. And we'll have to keep them isolated until the vet can check them out."

Luke lumbered up and his eyes about popped out as he looked from Blake to the Dane and pups. "Where are we going to put all these dogs?"

Mrs. Chantilly's face fell. "Mama and pups in the house. The side room on the right is empty now with all the adoptions. We put the first bunch in the room on the left. You were just in the garage. Is there room in there? Grandpa used to work out there so I think there's electric heat if we need it and a bathroom, too. Blake, how many more dogs?"

He pulled her close. "Remember, we need to keep these dogs separate from your other dogs. Let me check out the garage. We can always pull your car out. Work on getting them some food and water. Luke, come with me."

They disappeared. I turned to Mrs. Chantilly, "You stay with them. I'll go get water and start the bottles going."

As I walked into the house, I glanced down at the concrete floor, painted blue slate and sealed. At least if the dogs made a mess, there wouldn't be any damage. It was about an hour later when we finished relocating the Pets and Paws residents to the larger back room. The two new mamas and pups were situated on one side of the kitchen. They'd been bathed and fed and each family rested on a palette.

That left space in the other side room for any smaller dogs that might come in. If the new arrivals were medium to large dogs, we moved them to the unattached garage. They'd been fed and some had been bathed, now settled into crates. The heat was on and that at least took the chill off. Not exactly warm, but the dogs would all be out of the wind.

Blake hinted there still would be more dogs coming. With Mrs. Chantilly's blessing, I sent an email out to all the volunteers with a short note about the dogs coming in and needing assistance, if they were available. Whatever supplies were needed, starting with towels and blankets, I was confident Blake would take care of them.

CHAPTER 2

Blake wasn't kidding. It wasn't long before he was back with more dogs. I took a deep breath as a police cruiser and another car pulled in behind his SUV. We all stopped as Chief Peabody emerged from the cruiser. It was more than a little unusual for the chief of police to be involved with abandoned dogs, even this many. Yes, cruelty to animals was against the law, but it would likely only make his daily report. He stood tall and nodded to Blake and Luke as he approached Mrs. Chantilly.

"Morning, Dora. Looks pretty busy here with all these dogs from the old Stoneham place."

"Yes, Glenn. Did you come to help? Maybe your dog would like a playmate." Despite the smile on her face, her tone and the twitching of her fingers revealed her fear that was not the case. From his stiff posture and jaw, this was not a social call.

"I've got just about everybody from Clover Hill over to that house right now and checking the property. Nobody seems to know when the

8

Stonehams up and left and where all these dogs came from. Mess over there is worse than when your grandma had this place." He nodded toward her house as he spoke and cringed.

He looked at Blake, who had joined Mrs. Chantilly.

"You're right, Glenn. The Stoneham's kept to themselves even before the kids left and after Herman retired. Nope, they didn't socialize. I think I'm the closest neighbor and I never saw them, so I didn't miss them when they left. I feel badly about that."

Chief Peabody nodded. "We found an old backpack of Lacie's in the house. Any idea, Dora, how it might have gotten there?"

Mrs. Chantilly paled and Blake put his arm around her waist to steady her. "No. Lacie hasn't stayed with me for years. Maybe she donated it to Goodwill or something?" Lacie had been another instance when Mrs. Chantilly took in someone in trouble, though Lacie had lived with her for a while.

"Glenn, what's going on? We've got more dogs in need of care here and you're worried about an old back pack? Ask Lacie."

"Already did that. She doesn't recall what happened to it or when. The problem is, and we've called in the District detectives on this one, in one of the upstairs rooms, possibly a bedroom, we found a body. The ME's there now."

Mrs. Chantilly tottered and moaned, falling almost to the ground before Blake and I stopped her fall.

Luke suddenly appeared with a blanket. We managed to get her onto the blanket and wrap it around her. A woman I didn't recognize joined us. She was slim and didn't wait for anyone to give her directions. She knelt down and checked Mrs. Chantilly's pulse. "Water?"

Luke ran to get the water and returned in time to hear Mrs. Chantilly moan again. The woman took the water and raised Mrs. Chantilly's head so she could drink. As Mrs. Chantilly regained consciousness, she muttered, "Oh, no, Justine."

"Blake, we'll be over to your place to talk with everyone later today. These dogs had to have come from somewhere."

As he walked to his car, Melina's car pulled in with the kids. She waved to the chief as he left and looked to me with eyebrows raised in question.

"I saw the email and told the kids about it. They all wanted to help. What can we do?"

Mrs. Chantilly lamented, "The garage and side rooms. Bathing, feeding, and Vanna – Dr. Barksdale's here. So much to do. Where did Justine get all these dogs? How could she let them get like this?"

Mrs. Chantilly shook her head and Blake took her into his arms. There was much confusion for a few minutes, everyone trying to ignore Blake and Mrs. Chantilly. Unexpectedly, Luke was the one to take charge.

"Nedra and Maddie? There's a couple of mamas and pups. You're good with them and bottle feeding. They're in the side room like usual. Grab whatever you might need and try to get them settled in. Dr. H. already started the formula. The mamas need some help too."

The woman stepped in and addressed the girls. "I'm the vet, Dr. Vanna Barksdale. Let's go see what we can do to."

The girls nodded and Luke pointed them in the right direction. He cleared his throat and Blake turned, still holding onto Mrs. Chantilly.

"She needs to lay down. I'll take her in and get her settled, and then I'll be back to help." With that he propelled her toward the house. Melina looked from Luke to me.

"Most of the dogs brought here are in the garage. We need to bring the larger of these dogs down there as well. The smaller to medium dogs we can keep up here. They need baths, food, water, and some of them have ticks that need to come out. Doc Barksdale is going to be here for a while."

I nodded. "Luke and I have made some progress, but the ones we've already bathed and fed need to get out of the crates and do their business. We've no idea if they are even crate-trained – right now, they're too traumatized to object."

Melina nodded. "Let's get some coffee and get started. Maybe we can label each crate by how quickly they need to see Vanna. You know, like triage?"

Luke and I nodded agreement and headed for coffee and supplies. We found some ribbon in the kitchen supply closet left over from the holidays and took it with us. And then went to the dogs.

"You learned about triage as a kindergarten teacher?" That was Melina's full-time job.

She laughed. "No, from watching lots of medical shows and soap operas over the years."

Her older teen, Willie, was the only one of us who didn't know the routine. Luke oriented him and put him to work with the shelter's own dogs, who'd been neglected since the onslaught.

Blake stopped in briefly to get a list of what we needed for supplies. Mrs. Chantilly kept her house well-stocked, but not for this many dogs all at once. Sure enough, not long after, another batch of dogs were brought down to the garage. We'd run out of crates and had no choice but to put two dogs in the larger crates. Dr. Barksdale joined us after a while and looked around the area with a shake of her head.

Melina made introductions. "Hi, Vanna. I don't think you've met Sheridan Hendley. The ribbons aren't really for decoration here. We did a quick check and immediately noted the ones obviously in the worst condition. Those are the crates with red bows. The silver bow crates? Those dogs seem to be in better shape but still need to be checked out. The green bows mean we've already managed to get them bathed at least. If we spotted anything suspicious, there's a note on the top of the crate."

The vet exhaled. "Coffee?"

Luke walked in as she spoke. "I'll get coffees for all of us."

I heard him mutter, "Too bad there's nothing stronger in the house" and smiled. We all went back to work.

I wasn't too sure who arranged it or how, but I was sure thankful when someone announced there was pizza in the kitchen and soft drinks. It was then I realized just how exhausted I was. Usually, I volunteer for about an hour and this was going on three.

A hand printed notice in red with a hand drawn stop sign was posted outside the kitchen. "Use the bathrooms and wash your hands thoroughly with the antiseptic provided before entering the kitchen. Only wet hands allowed in the kitchen area."

I stuck my head in to see who was enforcing this and Willie cleared his throat. "Dr. Barksdale said to stop anyone who had dry hands. Sorry. You can't come in here."

He looked a bit sheepish, hands gripping the paper towels. Although only sixteen, he was a stocky young man, almost my height. I recalled Melina said he played football at Clover Leaf High. I smiled and headed for the bathrooms, running into Maddie and Nedra, hands out and dripping.

"No more paper towels, Sher. And Doc Barksdale said not to wipe our hands on our clothes."

"Willie has the paper towels in the kitchen and he won't let you in if your hands are dry. Better hurry up and get some pizza!"

I smiled when I realized Vanna Barksdale was monitoring the bathrooms to be sure everyone washed their hands. She hadn't mentioned anything contagious, so maybe she was just being careful.

Blake arrived with more supplies and took over helping with the dogs while we ate. Unfortunately, the media followed him. Although the reporters and videographers were kept at a distance, we could watch the broadcast of one perky young woman from WCLH on the small television in the kitchen while we ate.

Early this morning, Blake Buchanan, previously the Mayor of Clover Hill discovered dogs abandoned and neglected at the old Stoneham place. We're told more than twenty dogs have been rescued and brought to Clover Hill Pets and Paws. In fact, we just saw Blake Buchanan deliver ten large crates. No one knows how all those dogs ended up at the Stoneham place. There's some talk that Justine Stoneham was a hoarder and possibly hoarded stray dogs. Then apparently, she abandoned them. No one seems to know what happened to the Stonehams or when they left. We'll keep you posted and hopefully get some photos later today, as well as a report from Dr. Barksdale.

Mrs. Chantilly came into the kitchen and caught the broadcast. She was obviously upset by the report, tears running down her cheeks. Luke stepped in to comfort her and made her sit down and eat something. On the plus side, the media must not have known about the body.

Exhausted, I let everyone know my plans. "Maddie and I can only help for another hour or so. We need to take care of Charlie and Bella, and get dinner ready. Do we know if there are still more dogs coming in?"

"Vanna?"

I turned in the direction of Mrs. Chantilly's gaze. The vet had joined the group and was eating along with the rest of us.

"Everyone, listen up. Before I get to Sheridan's question, please take care when you go home, especially if you have pets. Just as a precaution, if you can change out of the clothes you've been wearing – your pants and top –before you enter the house, that is the safest. They should go straight into the washing machine. At the very least, leave your shoes off until you can spray them with disinfectant or bleach."

Maddie's hand went to her mouth and several others mouths dropped. Vanna continued.

"The last word I got as to whether there were more dogs was a big 'maybe' – they're still searching under the deck, some areas obstructed but with space a dog might fit through to get to shelter. Unfortunately, in moving some of the debris, they found some snakes and animal control had to come take care of them. They still haven't made it into all the rooms upstairs. Too much clutter and the men are not quite as slim as whoever lived there."

"How will they know when they've found them all?"

She shrugged and looked to the door where Blake now stood.

"They're trying to air the place out. Between the smell and the clutter, you couldn't even walk in the house without a mask. The dogs we found were still able to whine, howl or otherwise let us know where they were. Once we have the all clear, we'll bring my dogs back over to see if they can locate any others inside. The reason I came to find you, Vanna, I just got a call. There's one more mama on her way over and they're hoping she waits until she gets here to deliver."

Vanna dropped her plate and bolted out the door, almost running into Blake who had to move fast to get out of her way.

CHAPTER 3

It was still chilly, but we'd left our coats in the cars and didn't put them on over our clothes. Melina helped get all of Maddie's other stuff from her car. She, Nedra and Willie were leaving as well. We were all exhausted.

Brett texted as we were leaving. He'd seen the news. I let him know we were on our way home. At home, we went into the garage and I scrounged to find the bag of clothes for Goodwill so we could change. The clothes were a bit tight, not exactly fashionable, but served the purpose. Obviously, Bella and Charlie could hear us and welcomed us noisily through the door.

Showers done and laundry going, we collapsed on the couch. I didn't have the strength to cook dinner and Maddie had fallen asleep. I texted Brett, "Dinner. Take out?" He responded with a "thumbs up," which made me smile. Looking at Maddie, with Bella and Charlie curled up with us, I leaned back and rested my eyes.

The dogs woke us up when Brett pulled in the driveway. He'd picked up dinner from the Seafood Grill & Deli, one of our favorites. As we bustled around, Maddie filled him in.

"You should have seen all the dogs, Dad. It was amazing. And so many people there. Chief Peabody even came to help with the dogs and the veterinarian and Mr. Blake and some other people."

Her eyes brimmed as she continued. "The mamas were so thin and could barely stand up. The pups were hungry and Nedra and I kept feeding them and trying to keep track of who we fed and didn't."

She sniffed and then added, "Luke brought us some thick ribbons of different colors. We started tying a bow around the pups as we fed them. Nedra was gold and I was silver. One of them wouldn't eat and was really weak. He got a red bow. The vet took him away."

I had to admit, as much as I didn't trust Luke after his harassment of Maddie and other girls, as well as his involvement in various other illegal activities, he'd been indispensable today. Six months and an emergency seemed to bring out the best in him.

Brett took Maddie in his arms and shook his head. "You all did good deeds today. You helped the dogs and puppies. I bet some of them were cute, but not as cute as Bella, right?"

"Bella is the best." She immediately picked up Bella and loved on her. "I'm hungry. Can we eat?"

At Brett's raised brows, I responded. "Blake brought in pizza but that was several hours ago. I'm hungry, too and it looks like you got enough seafood salad, coleslaw, and fries for an army."

"Were you with the mamas and pups, too?" Brett asked as we each made a plate for ourselves and I grabbed the ketchup.

"I was in the garage dealing with the rest of the dogs. We also had to use ribbons to keep things straight. We haven't needed to see a vet since I've been here. I really liked Vanna Barksdale. She was efficient and friendly at the same time."

"Good to know. I guess at some point, Charlie and Bella will at least need their checkups and shots. I saw the media clips about the dogs."

"Yeah, the media hounds were at their usual best. Blake wasn't thrilled and banished them to the edge of the property. Although a shelter, he pointed out that Pets and Paws was private property. That at least got them out of the way. How was your day?"

"Nothing special." He shrugged. "And if it was, you'd see it on the news. Investigating tips about a possible car theft ring that may cross not only county, but state lines. The usual check on tips about drug trafficking. One questionable death that probably won't involve the State Police – ME hasn't determined cause of death or who the person is yet though."

He looked directly at me with the latter part and I caught on he was telling me what he knew.

"I see. Interesting. Are there any state or local laws on how many dogs one person can have or anything that might relate to the dogs?"

"There are some local ordinances about how many dogs can be in one house. Of course those vary from district to district. Mrs. Chantilly has a license to run the shelter and all the paperwork is filed and proper. Blake Buchanan saw to that. The Stonehams?

I don't know that they ever filed anything or even which district that property falls within or how the dogs ended up there."

Maddie chimed in, "Nedra and I tried to remember if there was anyone named Stoneham in our classes. She doesn't remember ever knowing anyone by that name. I guess they could go to the Academy."

"Melina didn't remember hearing about that family or knowing them. Blake said they kept to themselves. The kids had left the area some years ago – they'd be adults now. He didn't know everyone else left the area as well, and he's their closest neighbor. Maddie, do you remember when you looked up the history of Appomattox and Clover Hill – was there any mention of the Stoneham family?"

She shrugged. "I don't remember. That was a long time ago. I'll check tomorrow, though. I'm too tired tonight."

I nodded and we kept eating. When we'd looked at the history of the area before, the focus had been on the Buchanan family and their influence locally and beyond. Pretty impressive family power and Luke was Blake's grandson.

We cleaned up and Maddie excused herself to go watch a movie. Brett was about to say something when my phone chirped.

"Hi, Mrs. Chantilly. What's up?"

"Sheridan, you have to help me. Help Lacie. She works for the police department here, you know. Such a responsible person now. Not like she was before. Runaway. Her sweater. Her backpack. You have to help her. Like Luke."

I'd put the call on speaker as she started talking. From Brett's knitted brows, he didn't have any better understanding of what she wanted than I did.

"Mrs. Chantilly, I don't understand. What's happened to Lacie now?"

"Lacie's a good girl. People don't understand her, that's all. You know how it is. Still, teens need a helping hand. Dogs need training and care. They teach responsibility. Not what we saw today. Two more dogs went over the rainbow bridge this afternoon."

I cleared my throat. "Where is Lacie now?"

"She's at the police station, of course. She works there you know. Now, Glenn Peabody thinks she knows something about Justine's death. Of course, she doesn't. She was good with the dogs here. Understood the responsibility, bonded with them. Community service gave her the opportunity to learn to trust in animals, including the two-footed variety. Although I have to say, dogs are more loyal and trustworthy than humans most days."

I shrugged and Brett shook his head. Even after six months, I sometimes found it hard to make sense of Mrs. Chantilly's comments. All mixed up and not always with obvious connections.

"I'm planning to come in again tomorrow to help out with the dogs. We can talk then, okay?"

"Okay, Sheridan, I knew you'd help. So smart and savvy. And that husband of yours is certainly a hunk."

She disconnected immediately and I burst out laughing, both at her comment and Brett's open mouth, speechless upon hearing her last comment. She may be a little ditzy, but I agreed - my husband is a hunk.

CHAPTER 4

Brett was long gone and I was curled up with Charlie reading Cassidy Salem's latest mystery when Maddie woke up. Breakfast was waiting for her in the kitchen. She's grumpy most mornings, so I kept reading until she joined me.

"We're going to Pets and Paws today to help with all the dogs, aren't we?"

"Do you want to or did you have something else you wanted to do?"

"I want to help those dogs. There's no way Mrs. C. can get to all of them. Even with Luke helping."

I smiled, proud of her. "You're right, Maddie. Go get dressed and we'll go over there and see what we can do."

She nodded and disappeared into her room. Much more awake, she emerged, dressed in record time in jeans and a long sleeve tee. She rambled about school, her friend Alex, and the puppies. Meanwhile, I replayed the call from Mrs. Chantilly in my head. When we arrived, it seemed quiet compared to the prior craziness. We went in and Luke rushed past us with a quick "back in a minute."

Maddie and I ventured into the kitchen. In the remodel when Mrs. Chantilly took over, the cabinets became lockers and I stuffed our jackets and my purse in one of them. Surprised there wasn't any coffee made, I put on the pot. Too bad Mrs. Chantilly didn't have a Keurig. Luke joined us and sat down, winded.

"What's up, Luke? You look exhausted."

"That's an understatement. It wasn't too bad yesterday with all the extra hands and help and Doc Barksdale. Then everyone started to leave and all the dogs needed to go out and some obviously aren't house-broken or crate trained or strong enough to make it outside. I kept trying to make a chart of all the dogs and their needs…" He shook his head.

"We came to help. Did you or Mrs. Chantilly try to call Melina? Any of the other volunteers?"

He nodded. "Melina – and Nedra and Willie – are coming after lunch. Daisy and Susie should be here sometime this afternoon, assuming their flights got in on time. The other volunteers are still on vacation. They won't be back until Friday or Saturday." Daisy and Susie were two other volunteers who helped out a couple days a week.

Maddie's face lit up at the mention of Nedra. "Wait, I can call Alex and see if he can come help." At Luke's nod, she pulled out her phone and walked out of the kitchen.

"Where's Mrs. Chantilly and where do you need us to start?"

"She left early this morning and told me to 'carry on' and 'everything will be fine.' As if it was a normal day. She didn't say where she was going, but Lacie stopped by last night and then called first thing this morning. Lacie is a piece of work and Mrs. C. doesn't get it."

I nodded and then realization hit. He still had the same shirt and pants on as the day before and needed a shave. "Luke, have you been here all night? Did you get any sleep? Breakfast?"

He put his hands up. "I slept a couple of hours. As for breakfast, I'm hoping Mrs. C. brings some back with her. I finished the pizza last night."

He shook his head and drank the coffee I'd put on the table. After checking the provisions in the kitchen, I leaned out the door. Maddie was still on the phone.

"Maddie, is Angie going to bring Alex over?" Angie Champlin was Alex and Karla's mom, a nurse, and widow. Alex and Maddie had been on the short end of Luke's shenanigans during the summer.

At her nod, I continued, "Ask her to bring some breakfast food – Luke hasn't had breakfast and there's no human food here."

"She doesn't have to do that. I'll be fine."

I ignored him. "What can we do?"

He exhaled. "Maddie is great with the mamas and pups. She knows what to do. Nedra, too. If you can help with the others that would be great. I never finished with a listing and we don't have names. If you spot something the vet needs to see, they get a red ribbon like you were doing yesterday. She's supposed to be back later today. I'll check on the dogs in the back room."

I nodded and with coffee in hand went to the garage to see what I could do. It was overwhelming to see so many dogs, all looking needy. More than when I'd left the day before. Some yelping, some barking, some barely moving, one with a splinted leg. Luke had managed to assign a number to each crate and the clipboard indicated the last time the dog or dogs in that crate had food, fresh water, and gone out, and the last time the crate had been cleaned. I got to work.

By mid-morning, I needed more coffee and a few minutes of rest. Back at the main house, I found Luke snoring at the table, pastry and cereal on the table. Voices filtered in from the front door. Putting my finger to my lips, I diverted Mrs. Chantilly and a woman I guessed to be in her early thirties to the hallway.

"Shhh. Luke's asleep."

"It's so good to see you, Sheridan. Blake is a good boy. Luke, too. I know you all have it under control here. I'll have dog biscuits ready in no time. Did you know there's a nice young man in there with Maddie? So glad you're going to help Justine."

I started to ask if she meant Lacie and hesitated. She breezed right by me and I looked to the other woman. She was a little taller than me and slim, with brown hair pulled back tightly. Blue eyes and porcelain skin gave her an Asian appearance. She stood very straight, almost regal. Her face reflected no emotion as if what Mrs. Chantilly said made perfect sense.

"I'm Sheridan, a volunteer here. Did you come to help out with all the dogs?" I reached out my hand to shake and she stepped back. I withdrew my hand and worked at keeping a smile on my face.

She hesitated before she answered, not quite making eye contact. "I'm Lacie and yes, I'll help with the dogs. It's been a while, but I know the routine."

I couldn't help laughing. "Nice to meet you, Lacie, but with the sudden addition of all these dogs? Most in bad shape? There is no routine right now. The dogs from before yesterday are all here in the house, moved toward the back to accommodate all the mamas and pups and smaller dogs. Maddie and Alex are with them. The rest are down in the garage. Grab a coffee and it'd be great if you joined me down there."

"You don't need to tell me what to do. I don't need you or another mother. Stay out of my way and mind your own business."

I was stunned speechless. I turned around and grabbed another cup of coffee. So far, it looked like Luke's opinion of Lacie was right on. Then again, maybe I had come on a little bossy.

CHAPTER 5

Lacie darted ahead of me as I walked to the garage. The dogs all seemed happy to see us, though some barked or whimpered. After a brief explanation of the ribbon system and the clipboards, Lacie turned from me and I began with the crates with more than one dog. Thankfully, she took the hint and helped with the second dog as I took the first one out.

The dogs certainly seemed to like her and she did well with them. She whispered softly and I had no idea what she was saying, but it worked.

While we got the first crate cleaned up and the dogs back in, I tried conversation to no avail.

"Beautiful dogs, here. Hard to imagine someone letting them get in this condition."

"True."

"I'm relatively new here. Did you know the Stoneham family growing up?"

She tilted her head at me as if I had asked if she'd traveled to Mars yet. "They lived on the outskirts of town."

"It's a good thing Mr. Buchanan's dog found that puppy." I shook my head for emphasis.

"Are these all the dogs?" She looked around, her mouth flat.

"Mostly. I think maybe one or two went with the vet. Yesterday was the first time I met Dr. Barksdale. Come to think of it, when I was leaving she took off in a hurry – they'd found a mama about to deliver. I'm not sure what happened with her or the pups."

Her eyes glistened – the first real hint of emotion – and then she shook herself. "I think we'd best spread out and make sure we get to all the dogs."

With that she headed to the far right corner. I shrugged and went to the left. A few minutes later, Willie joined us.

"Hi, Ms. Sheridan. Mom'll be down in a few. Do you and Ms. Lacie want coffee?"

I chuckled. "Willie, you know I do. Ms. Lacie's over on the other side. You'll have to ask her."

He smiled and went off in her direction. The next thing I knew he was back with a tray and coffee for us, as well as bottled water. Melina followed with dog biscuits I suspected had just come out of the oven and donuts for the humans. Part sugar junky, I washed my hands and stopped working long enough to enjoy a donut and coffee. Willie joined me.

He glanced at Ms. Lacie and then cupped his hand as he stated, "That Ms. Lacie, I think she's a dog whisperer. One of the dogs was agitated and whimpering. She talked to him, real soft, and he immediately calmed down and let her take him out of the crate. Eerie."

I smiled. "Ms. Lacie used to help Mrs. Chantilly with the dogs before she started work at the police station. I think she probably developed a few tricks in the process."

As I watched her, I added to myself, "what she lacks in social skills with people, the opposite is true with the dogs." I wondered if she had a dog or two.

With four of us tending to the dogs, we managed to get the crates all cleaned, with water and food and clean "bedding," now limited to at least one towel. I noticed Melina try to engage Lacie in easy conversation and get the same brusque response I'd gotten. No big deal. The dogs all got some human time, and the ones strong enough got some play time outside.

We tagged only one dog for immediate attention by the vet. Lacie named her Rosie for her coloring and stayed with her, while Melina, Willie, and I went back up to the house. We heard the noise before we got in the door. Mrs. Chantilly and Chief Peabody and another officer I didn't recognize were at it.

"Now you listen to me, Glenn Peabody. I remember you from when you were in diapers. Do you know where your backpack from high school is? If Lacie says she gave clothes and the backpack to Goodwill, then she did. You made it out of diapers and she turned herself around. She's not the same hellion she was back then. Heck, you even hired her."

"Dora, we still need to talk to Lacie. Justine… someone had to have helped her. Her food was delivered to the house – ordered online. Justine didn't have a computer or smart phone. She had a land line and an old rotary one at that, not a portable one."

"What about Old Man Stoneham?"

"He's dead, buried in the backyard." He shrugged.

Mrs. Chantilly gasped and then took the offensive. "So, Justine killed him and buried him? Maybe his ghost came back to get her. Or the guilt could have done it."

"We're investigating his death as well. A ghost didn't kill Justine and didn't order her food to be delivered – including dog food. Last box was sitting inside the door, like someone brought it in and never got any further."

"That's the answer then. Justine brought the box in and some drifter surprised her from behind and killed her. Probably stole stuff, too."

Peabody and the other officer exchanged glances. "Dora, where's Lacie right now?"

"You two need to be figuring out where all these dogs came from and who killed Justine and Herman. We have work to do. Poor Luke was up all night, you know. He's passed out."

On cue, Luke stumbled into the doorway, not passed out yet barely awake.

"Mrs. Chantilly, we need to have a plan on re-homing these dogs." He looked to Melina and me. "If we get some pictures, can the two of you start contacting area shelters and rescues? Maybe they could take a few of them?"

"See, Glenn, we have a lot of work to do here." With that Mrs. Chantilly escaped to the second floor.

"Luke, that's a great idea. I can check out all the rescues. We'll start with the dogs that look the best. And maybe one of the mamas?"

Melina nodded agreement, then added, "Can you take the lead – technology and I don't always compute."

I nodded as Willie grinned and shook his head. "I'll go get a couple of pictures." He turned to Chief Peabody. "Shall I tell Ms. Lacie you want to see her?"

Peabody dragged his palm over his face and signaled to the officer. "No, son. We'll just go with you."

Melina, Luke and I watched them go. We weren't surprised when Blake arrived a few minutes later. Luke went to tell Mrs. Chantilly. Before we left, Willie sent me a bunch of pictures. As the police, Blake and Mrs. Chantilly started arguing again, we decided it was time to leave. I dropped Alex off at home with the same advice the vet had given us about changing clothes before playing with his own dogs.

CHAPTER 6

After showers and a quick lunch, I looked up rescues online reasonably close to Clear Leaf and sent off emails with photos and a lot of hope. Then I texted Brett we would be having dinner with the Champlins. I hadn't seen Angie or Karla in a while, so dinner would be fun. Tired out, both Maddie and I crashed. I'd just woken up and made coffee when Brett pulled in.

He gave me a hug and kiss before taking his coffee. "How were things at Pets and Paws?"

I gave him a quick summary, ending with the emails and photos I'd sent to rescues.

He nodded. "This will be on the news soon enough so I'll fill you in. The body was identified as Justine Stoneham, wife of Herman Stoneham. Blow to the head and left to die in a bedroom — boxes everywhere, almost obstructing the door. Even if she wasn't dead from the assault, she had no way to get help. The only phone was downstairs."

"Could she have fallen and hit her head?"

31

He shook his head. "From what I heard, there were boxes everywhere – in every room. Nothing that she could have hit her head on that hard. No indication of what or who hit her either. They can't be sure where she was when she was hit – she could have been hit in one place and then gone to her bedroom. It doesn't help that boxes and loose papers were moved to get to her and to get her out."

"Chief Peabody said they also found Herman's body?"

"There was no record of him leaving or where he might be. They searched as they need to notify next of kin. In the last round of checking for injured or sick dogs, with the help of one of Blake's dogs, they found a mound in the backyard. The dogs went crazy and they called in for shovels. They found Herman – or at least they think it was Herman – in his 'go to church' suit. No obvious foul play but the coroner is working on it. His initial guess was that Herman died about a year ago, maybe a little more."

I shuddered. "Did they have children? Was no one concerned they hadn't heard from them?"

"They had a daughter and a son. Best anyone can remember, they both moved away permanently after college. They have everyone they can find out there going through the papers and boxes to see if they can find a return address on a card or something."

He shook his head. "I stopped there on my way home. The smell… And it looks like they saved every bit of mail, junk and all, since forever."

"And the mail person didn't ever notice the smell or the dogs?"

"The mailbox is at the end of the drive with the house hidden at that point. Dogs barking? As long as they weren't coming after the person delivering mail and the mail was being picked up, why would they question it? Yesterday, the mail person noticed all the activity and brought the mail up —said two days of mail hadn't been picked up. The interesting thing is that somehow food was delivered – the most recent delivery was inside the door, delivered three days ago."

"Let me get this straight. Up until two days ago, Justine – or someone helping Justine – had collected the mail and the boxes of food. That means Justine was assaulted either three days ago on Saturday or Sunday after collecting the box and mail or on Monday, two days ago, before the mail came?"

Brett chuckled. "That sounds about right. Officially, the coroner will make that determination as well as cause of death. The question is whether Justine was the one collecting the mail and the box. If not and someone was helping her, who was it and why did they stop?"

"And where did all these dogs come from? Why didn't she or they get them the care and food they needed? This wasn't only two or three days of neglect."

The alarm on my phone sounded. "We need to meet Angie and the kids at Pizza Heaven in an hour. Good thing we like pizza. Time to get Maddie up."

We were running late and got to the restaurant later than planned. Thankfully, Angie and crew had been able to snag a table big enough for all us. I smiled when I saw Eric Pinsky.

Eric was an attorney who did a lot of pro bono work with adolescents. We'd gotten to know Angie and him when Alex and Maddie were implicated in a murder. He'd represented Alex then. He was single and did a lot of pro bono work. More and more, he was around when we got together with Angie.

"Hi, sorry we're late."

"No problem, Sheridan. Alex told us about the situation at Pets and Paws – I'm guessing you and Maddie took a nap, same as he did."

Angie reached over and tousled his hair. Alex in turn pulled away from his mom and shook his head. Angie and Melina were the two closest friends I'd made since moving. I smiled at the looks between Angie and Eric.

"We went ahead and ordered a couple of pizzas. Hope your tastes haven't changed any. Karla's sure she remembers what we had the last time." Eric looked over to her and smiled. Karla smiled back.

Alex was the first to bring up the dogs. "Have they figured out about the dogs and the woman they found?"

"Not yet. They're working on it. The dogs are doing better." I didn't bring up the second body.

"Luke was a big surprise. He was – well, human. Nice to me even and definitely working hard. After dealing with him last summer? Surprising to say the least."

Eric nodded to Alex. "Everyone deserves a second chance." He turned to me and asked, "So his probation with Mrs. Chantilly is working out, huh?"

I nodded and he continued, "I hear he's at Clover Hill High and not the private 'academy' now, too."

That surprised me and I wasn't sure how Eric knew that.

"What about Caleb? I haven't heard anything about his status." Caleb was involved in the harassment and activities in the summer as well, only he'd also developed a drug habit.

"Word is he's making good progress in rehab. The last month or so, he's been able to go home for a weekend with strict supervision and an ankle bracelet. With his uncle in prison, and his parents on board, he may be released from rehab. The hard part is finding community service for him. He made a lot of enemies in the past and not even Mrs. Chantilly is willing to take him on."

Angie shook her head. "I hope you kids learn from their mistakes."

"Where will all the dogs go?" Karla asked, her lips quivering. Eric patted her hand and looked at me, like I should have all the answers.

"Right now, we're checking with rescues in the general area to see if any of them can help out. I sent a few pictures and emails out." I shrugged. "A few of them had chips. Unfortunately Dr. Barksdale said the information was out of date."

Maddie bounced in her seat. "The puppies are so cute – though not as cute as Bella. Mrs. Chantilly is sure they will get adopted once they're healthy." As was often the case, the rest of the meal was taken over by talk of puppies.

CHAPTER 7

With only a few more days of winter break, I holed up in the shared room we called a home office to prep my classes for the spring semester. I liked working at Millicent College, but I still missed Cold Creek College and my friends there.

As if on cue, my best friend Kim called. We'd worked together for several years and had shared many experiences, good and bad.

"Hi, Kim. I was just thinking of you."

"We barely had time to catch up over New Year's but I'm so glad we were able to get together at all. More and more of my holiday time is with Marty's family."

"That's interesting. You good with that?" Kim didn't have a history of positive relationships though this one seemed promising. And I liked Marty.

"Oh, yeah. They've gotten used to me I think. And I to them. Are you ready for the semester to start? This call is my avoiding reworking syllabi."

We both chuckled. "That's what I'm doing this morning. Then I think we're going to Pets and Paws again. We've been spending a lot of time there the last few days."

"Marty mentioned the old lady who died with so many dogs left behind."

I filled her in on the dogs and Justine's death. A text message came as we lamented the plight of the dogs. "Kim, I'll have to call you back. One of the rescues I contacted just texted and asked me to call them."

"That's great! Hopefully, that will work out. In the meantime, you stay out of Justine's murder, if it is murder – Millicent College didn't seem too keen on your association with murder."

She laughed. But she was right. When Dr. Addison hired me, he'd made a comment about staying out of the news. I immediately called the number on the text.

"Fur-ever Home, good morning."

"Hi, this is Sheridan Hendley. I sent you an email and you texted me just now."

"Oh, yes. My name is Marcy Jenkins. I'm in charge here and… The large male, lab mix you sent a picture of? Please don't tell me that's Rosco. He was adopted out just a few months ago. Someone named Justine – please don't tell me he was abandoned again. We had a hard time finding a home for him because of his size."

My mouth dropped and I worked at coming up with an explanation. "I'm sorry to say Justine died and our local shelter took in all her dogs. I don't know if that is Rosco – there were no tags or collars on the dogs. I'll stop by today and see if the dog in this picture answers to that name. If so, can you take him?"

"I'm so sorry to hear she died, she seemed like a nice person. Elderly, you know. Like Rosco. Seemed like a great match. Do let me know if it's Rosco. In the meantime, I'll see if I can find a foster who could take him even if it's not Rosco."

"That would be great. Honestly, the shelter took in more than twenty dogs, not counting the mamas and pups. Any help would be appreciated."

"Oh my. The woman…she said she'd lost her husband and Rosco would be an only dog." She hesitated as she digested the lie and then suggested some other rescues in the greater Appomattox area. I jotted them down.

After sending a few more emails with the pictures we'd taken, I worked on my syllabi until Maddie got up. Both our dogs fed and taken for a short walk, we left for Pets and Paws.

Mrs. Chantilly greeted us before we reached the front door. "Sheridan, Maddie. It's so good to see you again. Isn't the weather beautiful? Too soon we'll have snow again. Chloe and Buster love playing in the snow. We have to have another adoption day. They so need a forever home."

"Good morning, Luke. Did you manage to get some sleep?" Luke nodded. He looked much better.

"Yes, ma'am, I did. I feel better, and so thankful for you and Maddie and the others." He shook his head with a side glance to Mrs. Chantilly.

"Susie's back today to help as well." He gestured in Susie's direction and I almost laughed at her wide eyes. A technician with one of the local veterinarians, she was mature and capable. And obviously stunned. She looked to Maddie.

"I need some help with all these mamas and pups."

That was all it took and Maddie was off chatting away with Susie.

"I'll just grab some coffee and go see what the status is in the garage."

"Have you solved the mystery yet? I know you can do it. You're not going to get any help from Lacie, you know. She doesn't open up to people, only dogs. You will help her won't you and prove she didn't kill Justine. I know you will. Justine was a little odd, you know. It must have been a drifter. It will all work out, won't it Luke?"

By the time I worked out the substance of what she said, she disappeared. Luke shrugged.

"She'll make biscuits now. There are one or two more dogs in the garage – Dr. Barksdale brought them in last night. Another one with a broken leg - Horatio. We also had an owner surrender last night – tied the dog to the porch railing, rang the bell, and drove off. She's in the back room. I'm going to take care of them and then I'll be down to the garage."

I nodded and grabbed a cup of coffee before I made my way to the garage and the dogs there. Lacie was already at work.

"Hi, Lacie. How's it going?" I tried my best to be friendly.

She shrugged. "Okay. Luke and I moved the crates around. Organization is key. I started on this side. You start on that side. When either of us gets to a crate with multiple dogs, we can both take care of those."

I looked around and noticed the crates were a little less scattered, more in neat rows, smaller crates with one dog along the wall. The larger crates with multiple dogs were in the middle.

"Sounds good. Luke said he might be down in a bit as well."

"Whatever. Just stay out of my business, you hear."

I nodded and focused my attention on the dogs. The dog in the picture wasn't where I remembered him. I wandered down the aisle between crates, looking for him, and softly called, "Rosco? Rosco?"

One dog, the one in the photo, barked and climbed the side of the crate. I went to him, and comforted him. "Rosco, I think we may have a home for you." He licked my hand, his tail wagging.

I looked around and caught Lacie watching. She turned away and didn't say a word. I marked Rosco's name and the name of the rescue on the crate's clipboard. Having already gotten him excited, I took him outside and then made sure he had food and water. Thankfully, his crate was clean. After marking the time, I went back to the start of the aisle, to be sure nobody was missed.

My watch alarm went off after a while. "Lacie, I'm not sure what's holding Luke up. I have to leave for a while, Maddie has an appointment, but I'll be back later. The dogs all look so much better."

She nodded and then turned away. It was disheartening to see all these dogs, some in appalling shape. Up at the house, I prompted Maddie about the time and looked for Luke.

"Mrs. Chantilly, I'll be back in a while, but I have to take Maddie to choir practice. Remember I took some pictures and was going to email them to nearby rescues?"

"Rescue. I don't like that word. Some places just take your money and don't care about dogs at all. Like children who grow up. Happy and sad at the same time to see them go. Like Lacie. Luke, too. Sad but glad."

"Mrs. Chantilly, someone at Fur-ever Home recognized one of the dogs. His name is Rosco and she's checking to see if his foster family can take him back. Isn't that great?"

"Too many dogs. We need more help and people to take them. Many fosters keep the dogs forever, you know."

I nodded. Maddie nudged me. "We gotta go. I'm going to be late for choir rehearsal."

"See you later, Mrs. Chantilly."

"Bye, Mrs. C."

In the car, Maddie chattered on and on about the puppies. I nodded, still thinking about Rosco and Justine getting him from a rescue. Maybe that was how she ended up with all these dogs. I pulled into the parking lot at the middle school. As Maddie catapulted out of the car, I yelled, "Have a good time. I'll pick you up in two hours."

The more I thought about it, the more I was sure Chief Peabody should hear about this. Sitting in the parking lot, I called him before calling Marcy to confirm it was Rosco.

"Chief Peabody, please, this is Sheridan Hendley and I may have information on the dogs over at the Stoneham place." I smiled to myself. If this was a big city, there's no way I'd ever be talking to the chief, but in this small district and with two bodies, he was pretty hands on.

"Chief Peabody here."

"Hi Chief, this is Sheridan Hendley. I've been working over at Pets and Paws and sent out a few photos of the dogs to nearby rescue groups to see if any could help. There are way too many dogs for Mrs. Chantilly to handle. Anyway, I know I'm rambling, but one of the rescues got back to me. She recognized the dog as Rosco and said Justine adopted him from her rescue. Maybe that's where all these dogs came from – rescues."

"That's interesting. I'll have someone follow up on that, Sheridan. Do you have the number?"

I gave him her name and number. "I'm about to call her to let her know it is Rosco. Should I mention someone from the police might call her?"

"That would be good. Let her know we may want some additional information so she isn't surprised. And thanks, Sheridan. Let me know if you find out anything else."

Even though he couldn't see me, I smiled at the phone as he disconnected. Then I called Marcy and confirmed it was Rosco. I smiled again when she shared that the foster would take him back as soon as he was cleared by the vet. I promptly gave her Dr. Barksdale's number.

I made a quick stop at the grocery store. After putting the bags in the trunk, I got in the car and groaned. Someone had written something on my windshield. I had to get out of the car to read it and looked around. MYOB was the message. I tried to wipe it off and realized it was soap. I couldn't drive the car without cleaning it off so I took a picture. The windshield wiper fluid did a fair job – enough for me to drive next door to the carwash. Later that night, I showed the picture to Brett.

"Not good. At least no permanent damage or threat. I seem to recall someone telling you that recently?"

"Lacie. At least twice. I'm pretty sure she stayed behind to help with the dogs. I didn't see her in the store or in the parking lot. And it's not like whoever did it left the bar of soap for fingerprints or we could get fingerprints off the soap if they did."

Brett shook his head. He knew that wouldn't stop me from helping out at Pets and Paws.

CHAPTER 8

It was the last weekend before back to school for Maddie and meetings for me. Pets and Paws would have to wait. We'd already planned skating with Alex, Karla and their mom, Angie, in the morning. Not Maddie's best time of day, but the skating rink wouldn't be as crowded in the morning.

As we pulled up, and Karla got out of their car and maneuvered her walker, I hoped this would work. Angie must have caught my worried expression before I smiled.

"We try to expose her to everything any other girl her age does. The cerebral palsy is mild and she can do a lot with the walker."

I nodded, still not clear how the walker would work on ice. Karla, on the other hand was as excited as Maddie and Alex. Inside we all got skates.

A young man came out to join us as we all got our skates on. He was taller than Alex with a more athletic build. He looked to be the same age as Luke or Willie. My best guess was a sophomore in high school.

"Hi. I'm Dan. I understand we have a new skater who may need some assistance."

I'll give him credit. He looked around our group until Karla raised her hand. "Me. I've... I've never been on skates."

"Okay then. Let me get you started. Take my hands and see if you can stand up on the skates."

Karla took his hands and, with help from Angie, she stood up. "Ready? Now lock your hands around my forearms. Don't look at your feet. Keep your eyes on my face. We'll take a spin around the rink. You'll have to be my eyes and tell me if I'm heading for the wall or about to skate into someone."

Her initial wide-eyed expression with clenched teeth erupted into a smile, as he slowly pulled her forward and propelled her around the rink. Maddie and Alex joined them, Alex pulling Maddie. Brett stood and put out his hands and we did likewise.

I looked over wondering about Angie alone and smiled. Eric had joined her and was skating up. I was glad to see their relationship was moving forward.

There were only a few other kids and no one was skating wild. Some even copied our tandem skating. After a few trips around the rink, Dan skated up to us with Karla.

"I'm afraid I need to get back to the hut – the line is getting long, and I left Sam there all by himself."

I looked at Brett and he gave me a slight push off. I stepped in behind Karla while Dan and Brett made the trade-off. We skated for about an hour more, though Karla tired quickly and sat out after a while.

Alex and Maddie could have skated longer and it sure looked like Eric was born on skates. The rest of us were cold and tired. In the hut, we all had hot chocolate. Dan delivered them and joined us for a minute.

"Dan lives out by Mr. Buchanan and the lady who died." Karla offered.

"Yeah, it's really sad she died. Until a couple of months ago, she'd have me come out and clean up the yard, mow the lawn. You know, the things she couldn't do. With winter, I haven't been out since before Halloween."

Brett cleared his throat. "Dan, did you notice a lot of dogs or a dog run or anything?"

He smiled and his face lit up. "Oh, yeah. She had quite a few dogs – maybe five or six that 'helped' me with the yard work. Chased me on the mower and stuff. Rosco was my favorite. Sometimes he was inside, sometimes outside."

"And the dogs all seemed healthy?" I asked.

"Oh, yeah, more or less. Food and water were always on the porch. Maybe in need of a bath." He laughed. "One time I was there was after a heavy rain. They kept jumping in the muddy water. I offered to try and dig a small trench or something to divert the water into the woods. Mrs. Stoneham, she told me not to, that there were bad spirits if I got too close to the woods. She always had me stop mowing and raking at the same place. Somehow the dogs knew to not go into the woods there, too."

Not wanting to make a big deal, I held my tongue and didn't ask for a better description of where the bad spirits were. We'd have to let Chief Peabody know to talk to Dan and he could get the specifics.

Hot chocolate finished, we all left to go in separate directions. My plan was to go help out at Pets and Paws for a few hours, and then to finish my syllabi. When my phone rang and I saw the caller ID, I choked.

"Hi, Kim. How are you?" I looked at Brett. From his dropped mouth and head shake, I wasn't the only one who had forgotten our dinner plans.

"I'm great. Marty called and he's stuck helping his sister with something. It's always something. Anyway, we probably won't get to your place until just before 6 p.m. Is that okay? Honestly, I can't remember what time our reservations are for."

"We're in the car on our way home. I'll check when I get home. I can always call and see about 6:30 so we aren't all rushed."

"Great. I can't wait to see you and Brett and Maddie."

"Same here. We'll see you in a few hours."

I disconnected and looked over to Brett. He was shaking his head and smiling at the same time.

"Completely forgot about it and I guess you did, too. Good bluff."

"Yup. I think I made those reservations before Christmas. Hopefully, I wrote it down on the kitchen calendar. I checked my phone while she was talking and it isn't on my phone calendar."

Although we were pretty well digital and smart-phoned, our feeble attempt at trying to use a family e-calendar and personal ones ended up with appointments missed or both of us going to pick up Maddie.

With Maddie's schedule and activities, as well as our own, we opted for an old-fashioned calendar in the kitchen with everything for everybody. Whoever was involved in an activity then added it to their calendar. Obviously, we'd both missed this one.

"Remember me? It's not on my phone either. Am I going? Or staying home alone?" Maddie paused barely and her voice raised in pitch. "Can I call Nedra and see what she's doing?"

Brett laughed. "It's just dinner and I think at thirteen you can handle being alone for a couple of hours, but you can certainly check with Nedra."

"After we change, we can go to Pets and Paws for a little while. Melina's helping out today and Nedra is probably there too."

CHAPTER 9

Before we left for Pets and Paws, I checked my email and found responses from some more shelters. The ones I'd sent pictures to thought they recognized a dog or two. I printed them all out. It was easier to respond to them when I was there with the dogs.

One other response suggested three other smaller rescues that might have space. I was feeling more optimistic about the situation until we got there. Maddie and I could hear the yelling from outside.

"You just leave Lacie here. She's good with the dogs and they'll help her learn responsibility and empathy. You'll see. She'll grow up to be a good citizen."

"Dora! Mrs. C! I'm standing right here all grown up. Stop talking about me like I'm not here. You were always a little odd, but you're losing it."

"You don't understand. We need to get Dr. Barksdale back out here for Rosie. Hi Sheridan, Maddie. Isn't the weather grand today? It won't last and we'll probably get some snow later this week.

Always hard on the dogs, though some of them seem to like to play in the snow."

I pushed Maddie in the direction of the mamas and she darted away from the chaos. Mrs. Chantilly turned to walk away and Chief Peabody opened his mouth. "Dora?"

She turned back. "And Glenn, please give my best to your wife. Are you sure you wouldn't like a dog? We have some beautiful pups and Dr. Barksdale says they're mostly all healthy. Now everyone get to work. Luke can't do it all and I need to tend to the biscuits."

She smiled and once again reminded me of a Mrs. Claus. Although I'm a psychologist, I never was quite sure she intentionally ignored or added content, or as Lacie put it was "losing it." The chief grimaced.

In the lull, I interjected, "Before you get busy with the biscuits, I heard from some more shelters. Okay if I give them calls when I see which dogs are ready to be placed?"

"Wonderful and we can have an adoption day and hopefully get all these beautiful creatures re-homed in a week or so. I have to admit, there's no more room in this inn and my babies are suffering."

She glanced at the back room where the long-term dogs were currently housed and her eyes teared up. She was right about one thing – the longer the dogs stayed at Pets and Paws, the more attached she became. I wondered how long Lacie had stayed with her.

Lacie stormed off toward the garage. Peabody looked at me and shrugged. "Getting any information is … I gather you may have some though."

I handed him the printed emails. "I'm not sure this has anything to do with Justine's or Herman's deaths though."

"I'm not sure either. Ms. Jenkins from Fur-ever Home told me Justine went to where Rosco was fostered and picked him up – by herself. I talked to the foster mom and she definitely described Justine. She said Justine took to Rosco immediately – she was sure he'd found his 'forever' home. And she gave us the date and Justine's phone number, which matches the land line at the Stoneham place."

"Did Justine have a car? She was driving places to get these dogs?"

"Her driver's license was up to date and she had a car – a beat up old SUV 2000. It's registered to Herman."

"Was there anything interesting in the car?" I hoped there weren't dogs left in the car in the cold.

Peabody's eyes got wide. "I don't know that anyone checked the car other than to verify it belonged there. On that now. Let me know what you find out about these." He handed me back my printouts.

"One more thing. You might want to talk to Dan who works at the skating rink. He told us he was helping Justine with upkeep until Halloween."

His eyes widened again and he nodded. In the kitchen, I fixed a cup of coffee and called the shelters that indicated they might have space to get some details. Each call was the same. Only one got me excited.

"Ms. Walker, this is Sheridan Hendley. I emailed you about some dogs here in Clover Hill that we need some help with."

"Oh, yes. I got your email. You indicated the shelter had taken in a large number of dogs that had been abandoned."

"Yes, ma'am. An older lady passed away. I don't think she planned to abandon them."

"Can we possibly FaceTime and you could show me some of the dogs? That might be easier than trying to identify all the breeds and mixes."

"That's a great idea. I'll walk down to where they're housed right now and call you back."

At the garage, Lacie was on the floor with one of the dogs. She turned so her back was to me when I came in. I shrugged and called Ms. Walker back using FaceTime.

After confirming that she could see the dogs, I stopped at each cage and gave her basic information. At one of the larger cages with two dogs – beagle mix was my best guess – she gasped.

"Beautiful, aren't they? There's a note here that says they are a pair and should not be separated if possible." I had no idea how anyone would know that unless they'd already tried to separate them.

"Paisley and Plaid. I recognize them. Where did all these dogs come from?" Her voice broke as she spoke. The dogs danced at their names.

"An elderly woman. As I mentioned, she passed away."

"We try so hard. We meet them, you know, when they come to adopt. It must be almost a year ago when they were placed. We can't do background checks or visit everyone's home. We're mostly concerned if it looks like the person might use them for bait dogs. I remember her, she was so kind."

"I know. Ms. Walker, can you call one of them? I'll try to figure out how to differentiate them."

She chuckled. "No need. Look at the paws. Plaid's paws are black, brown and white, almost in stripes. Paisley's are black and brown with only a smidgeon of white breaking it up."

I studied their paws and smiled. Other than the paws, these two girls looked identical. Who needs fingerprints with such different paws? "I'll make a note on that. Any chance you could take them back?"

"I will once they're cleared there and here. I'm pretty sure I know a foster. Are you able to give me the name of the person who passed away? I'm part of a group of shelter owners and I can post and see if anyone else adopted out to this person – assuming she used her real name, of course."

"Justine Stoneham. If you could let them know to contact Chief Peabody here in Clover Hill, I think he'd like to know."

After giving her Peabody's number, I finished the walk through. Lacie had disappeared and Luke had come in. He'd listened to the commentary and gave me a 'thumbs up' when he realized what I was doing. He was more alert than the day before, but still tired. And school would be back in session on Monday – only one more day of lots of help at Pets and Paws.

He walked over as I disconnected. "Any luck?"

"One rescue said they'll take Paisley and Plaid for sure – the two beagles over there. She recognized them. She'll see if she can make room for at least a couple more of the smaller ones. One way or the other, she'll come by tomorrow afternoon and take as many as she can find fosters or has room for. I don't see Rosco. Did Marcy Jenkins come for him?"

"Yeah. Yesterday." He laughed. "You'd have thought we'd given the boy a steak. He was sure glad to see her."

I cringed as I realized how little time I had to help. "Which ones need the most right now? I only have about an hour left."

CHAPTER 10

It was perfect timing. Nedra arrived as we finished getting dressed. A few minutes later, Kim and Marty arrived. After hugs with Maddie and introductions, we were on our way to dinner. The Steak Place was the closest nice restaurant, and reservations were a must. On the other hand, it didn't look fancy or different than what anyone would expect from a steak place. Lots of wood and simple.

"Sure smells good. I'm hungry."

Kim poked Marty. "You're always hungry. But you're right. The smell makes my mouth water."

"We've eaten here before and the food definitely tastes as good as it smells."

Brett nodded in agreement and then moved forward to speak with the hostess. After we were seated, I asked, "Kim, what's happening with the Department Head position?"

Jim Grant, the Department Head at Cold Creek College either decided to retire or was told to, so there would be a new person in charge by next fall.

When I left, Kim became the unofficial Assistant Department Head.

"I told you Max was applying, right? He's convinced he'll get the job. He tries to tell Ali and Terra what to do and they remind him he doesn't have the job yet. He was hard to live with before but now? Unbelievable."

Max was overly enthusiastic and highly excitable. He'd shown that he had a heart of gold, but most of the time he wore us out and made us crazy. A bit condescending and erratic, he was hard to deal with. I chuckled as I pictured him with his black hair, always mussed and sticking out, chasing his rats when they escaped his cages. He'd certainly lost it if he thought he could tell the two administrative assistants what to do. Ali and Terra were indispensable in the department.

"Has he come up with a plan to put more emphasis on research?"

Kim snorted. "He tried. Met with the Chancellor believing he was going to be the impetus to change the sleepy little four-year college into a research university. Only he apparently didn't realize that it cost the college money every time he submitted grants – five that didn't get funded, mind you. The Chancellor put a kibosh on his plan and told him to stop wasting money on grant applications."

I shook my head. "I bet he was fuming and sad all at the same time. I'm surprised he didn't push harder to go to one of the bigger universities. He always talked of doing that. I feel bad he can't realize his dream."

Kim hesitated. "Terra got mad at him, his 'I'm so much better than you' attitude and his attempts to bully her into doing things. She put him in his place. Apparently, he had her generating the cover letters or addressing the envelopes or something for positions all these years. She ranted on in front of anyone around about how many positions he's applied for in the past few years, every year."

We all grimaced. No one would want that kind of information shared. As key staff in the department, Terra had a strong personality for sure. She wasn't hateful though and he must have really pushed her limits.

Our food arrived and conversation stalled, replaced by sounds of pleasure, smiles, and nods at the great food. I was ready to ask about other news from Cold Creek, when Marty asked a question.

"Kim filled me in a little and, of course, I heard about the bodies and all the dogs... What's the latest on that?"

I looked at Brett and he nodded. "There were more than twenty dogs found in various states of health. And some others that didn't make it. That doesn't count at least four mamas and pups. Another mama went straight to the vet clinic." As I spoke, I realized I hadn't heard the status on them.

"We're trying to find rescues to take some of the dogs. Mrs. Chantilly is convinced the pups will be adopted easily and she's probably right."

"And the bodies?" I turned to let Brett answer Marty's question.

"The woman appears to have been hit on the back of the head and subsequently died. The man, her husband, was found buried in a shallow grave in the backyard. You may not know this yet, Sheridan, but the coroner concluded that he died of natural causes.

No indication of foul play and every indication of heart damage. He was buried in his Sunday go-to-church suit. Best guess was about a year or so ago."

"How did she manage to dress him, carry him to the backyard, and bury him?"

"Good questions. The only explanation is that she had help. She was thin and shorter than him. No one thinks she could have dragged him any distance."

"How old were these people? Old enough to collect social security?" Marty asked, his finger on his chin.

"In their seventies. I think he worked all his life and may have had both social security and a retirement account." Brett shrugged. "They're looking into the finances and how bills were paid. Not sure what they've found so far."

Marty nodded. "I'm not an estate attorney or financial wizard by any means, but here's my thinking."

He hesitated. "As long as no one knew the man was dead, the checks would still be issued – whether from retirement or social security or both. If he was a veteran, he'd possibly get still another check. That could be motive for keeping his natural death a secret. His wife might have thought she'd make out better with the monthly checks than with the payoff at the end, what with taxes and all. Anyone look at the tax return for last year and the year before? How'd he sign it if he was deceased?"

Brett nodded. "All questions the chief is going to have to deal with. What with the bodies and dogs, I'm not sure anyone has gotten far in looking at finances. I saw pictures of the inside of the house."

He rolled his eyes for effect. "Boxes and books and papers stacked as high as Maddie is tall in some places. Barely enough room to walk and a maze to get from one room to another. And I stopped by. The smell? Bad doesn't even begin to describe it."

Kim shuddered. "I heard she was a hoarder. Hoarding is associated with anxiety and depression. It probably got worse after her husband passed."

We were all silent. Discussions of death and mental illness can have that effect. The waiter came with the dessert menu and that seemed to cheer us up. Apple pie with vanilla ice cream all around.

"Next time it's our turn to come to Cold Creek."

"I know it's not far off, but how about the third Saturday in February? We can go to North Shore like old times?"

"As long as we don't get hit with snow storms, that sounds good. I miss hanging out with you guys."

I'd made some friends in the past six months. It wasn't quite the same though, not yet. This time the dinner date went on both our phones.

CHAPTER 11

The phone ringing woke me out of a sound sleep. Calls early in the morning or late at night always gave me a sense of foreboding. "Hello?"

"Sheridan. Chief Peabody here. Sorry for the early call, but I wanted to catch you before church. Would it be okay to stop by after lunch? I'd like your opinion on something."

"Morning, Chief. I think we'll be here around lunch time and early afternoon." Brett nodded, his head cocked to the side.

"I'll see you then." He disconnected.

"What did he say?"

"He wants my opinion on something?" I shrugged. "He sounded cryptic."

Brett grunted. "Guess we might as well get up. No telling what he wants you to look at."

He made breakfast as I showered. We talked more about Justine, Herman, and the dogs. Online I found a newspaper clipping of the Stonehams at some church event five years ago. Herman was a stocky man, not tall, yet much taller than the petite woman at his side. According to the brief article, he retired at age 67 and this was a celebration. Maddie appeared as I shared this with Brett.

"Did you find anything else about them?"

"No. I stopped when I found this. Have some breakfast."

She ate and quickly volunteered to see what else she could find. I smiled and Brett shook his head. "I guess we get to do the cleanup – again."

I smiled as I picked up the breakfast dishes. Once they were done, Brett was ready to run out and get what we still needed for dinner and Maddie came running.

"You'll never believe this. There was a big rivalry in the past between the Buchanans and the Stonehams. I found stuff on fights between the families. I think it must have been Mr. Blake's grandparents or something. It's all fuzzy and hard to read."

She handed me a print out and it certainly fit with what I'd expect from the early offset printing presses. I passed it to Brett, thinking it was not surprising Blake didn't know what was going on over there. Maddie continued to explore, ignoring my directions to get the laundry done.

Brett left with the grocery list and I disappeared into the home office to work on my courses. The morning flew by and I jumped when Brett returned.

"Lots of talk going on about the Stonehams. I got the feeling the family was not well accepted in Clover Hill. No one seemed to know why and it didn't seem to be specific to Justine and Herman. Odd, don't you think?"

I nodded. "Why would one family be ostracized to such an extent? Herman obviously worked and they must have gone to church, at least as of five years ago for that event. Didn't anyone notice when they weren't there?"

Brett shrugged and massaged my shoulders. I felt a melancholy sinking in. The mood shifted with the doorbell. "I'll get it."

Brett nodded and added, "And I'll check on Maddie."

I opened the door and found Chief Peabody holding a box filled with paper, crumpled and messy paper.

"Hi Chief. Come on in."

"Thanks, Sheridan. I can tell from your wary expression you figured out what I need help with."

"All that paper?"

He nodded. Brett joined us as he explained.

"This is all the paper we found in the Stoneham SUV – well, maybe not all of it. Some of it was too, uh, soiled to salvage. There are emails and flyers and announcements. Many related to animal shelters and rescues. Since you're helping identify rescues to take the dogs in, I figured… Could you sort through this and identify anything that seems important for me to follow up on? There are pictures of dogs and you may recognize some of them."

He exhaled and waited for my answer.

"I'll do what I can. Did they have a computer? A printer?"

He shrugged. "Not that we've found so far. If you find anything I might need to see, please put those aside and give me a call. Otherwise, at least you may find some additional places to call to re-home dogs."

I nodded. "Do you know anything more about them? How she was killed? Who helped her bury Herman?"

"I had a long talk with the pastor at the small church in the south of town, Pastor Pete. He called and asked about funeral arrangements. He said Herman and Justine were church-goers. He wondered what happened to them, but they didn't tend to share information. Kept private most of the time. The pastor said they usually made church at least a couple times a month, then stopped. Pastor guessed the last time he saw Herman or Justine was about over a year ago."

The chief chuckled as he continued. "The pastor laughed as he told me, 'Herman always wore the same suit, with the mustard stain on the lapel. Man did like mustard on his hot dogs.' The pastor's time frame fit with the coroner's and the way he was dressed in the suit. Still, Herman was twice the size of Justine. Someone had to have helped her dig the shallow grave and lay him to rest. Why didn't she tell anyone?" The chief shook his head.

I shrugged, pretty sure the answer was not in the box of papers. Brett walked the chief out. At the kitchen table, I started to glance through the stack and gasped.

"What? Did you find something already?"

"Brett, look at this. These emails are to Lacie; she must have printed them out and given them to Justine."

He shook his head. "Not looking good for her. See if you can find anything else before we call him. I'm going to check on Maddie and the laundry."

I spent the next hour weeding through the stack of paper, separating flyers from emails. The flyers didn't indicate where they were printed. The emails did. Two different email addresses for Lacie on two different mail services.

The flyers were all inviting people to come view dogs ready for their forever homes. I recognized Paisley and Plaid right off. The emails asked for information on dogs seen on social media and if they were still available, and who to contact. Most of these were more than six months old.

The email with Rosco's foster home was the most recent. When I was done, I had the emails for forty-five different rescues or foster homes, only eight of which I had already contacted. I finished sending the last email to the new ones when Brett cleared his throat.

"You about done there? Maddie's ready to go shopping and use her Christmas money from my mother and yours."

"I'm done. This is amazing. Unbelievable. Could one person really set out to adopt forty-five dogs? Her hoarding extended beyond the stuff in the house. She hoarded dogs, potentially as pets, but unable to care for them. With all the people helping at Pets and Paws these last few days, we had trouble making sure they got what they needed. No way could she care for them."

I shuddered. "How'd she think she could take care of all these dogs, see to their needs? It's disturbing on so many levels. Give me a few minutes to call Chief Peabody and fill him in. Maybe we can drop off my spreadsheet and return all this to him at the same time."

"Give him a call and I'll fix lunch. At least by now everyone will have already completed all the gift returns. It shouldn't be too crowded." To say shopping was not Brett's favorite thing would be an understatement.

A brief phone call, lunch eaten, spreadsheet printed, and we were on our way. Maddie found two nice sweaters in record time, and we left the box with the chief. Then Maddie modeled the sweaters with Facetime for each of the grandmothers. They were thrilled.

CHAPTER 12

Brett off to work and Maddie to school, Monday was to be my day to work on the courses I'd be teaching at Millicent College spring semester – I had one more week. I planned to work until noon and then go over to Pets and Paws for a few hours to help out and share the news from my emails. Several of the shelters confirmed Justine had adopted a dog or a pair of dogs. They were most willing to take the dogs back once the vet cleared them.

I was so engrossed, I jumped when the doorbell rang, not expecting anyone or anything. A quick check and it was Chief Peabody.

"Hi Chief. Come on in."

"Thanks, Sheridan. I hate to bother you, but you seem to have a good head and Hirsch had a lot of positive things to say about your ability to make connections. Plus, you have the advantage of not being overly familiar with all the parties. I need some objective input, if you wouldn't mind."

I smiled as I thought of Hirsch, the chief back in Cold Creek and a friend. "Happy to be of help, if I can. Coffee? I have some cinnamon coffee cake, too."

"That would be great, but don't go to too much trouble. I have to tell you, I'm not sure where to start."

"It might help if you could give me some background on Herman and Justine and the rest of the Stoneham family."

"Okay, but that's not as easy as it sounds. I touched base with some of the elderly citizens. It seems several generations back there were some issues regarding the land and where the boundaries were between the Buchanan and the Stoneham properties. The records show that a line was drawn and codified that separated the two large plots of land, and at the same time put the Stoneham property outside of Clover Hill jurisdiction."

"What does that mean? On a practical level at least?"

"It means that accessing any services was not automatic. In order to have access to water, sewer, electric, and so on, there were additional fees attached. There were also some questions as to whether police or fire from Clover Hill would cover the property."

My mouth dropped and he held up his hand.

"At some point later, that was all straightened out with Herman's grandfather signing off on the next document. Herman was the only son of an only son. I found no record of where Herman or his father went to school, probably private. Herman attended a private college and got a degree in finance. He came back to the area, lived in the family home until his parents died, and worked in the main office of the bank in Appomattox."

"Isn't that a long commute?"

He took a drink of coffee and a bite of the coffeecake. "About twenty minutes. Not bad, really. About the same as for Brett."

"And Justine?"

"There's less in our records about Justine. Justine and Herman married in their late twenties. Her maiden name was Hartfelt. No criminal record. First driver's license was issued in Roanoke."

He shrugged and then continued. "They had two children, Jacob and Helen. They all lived in the house that had been in the Stoneham family for generations with Herman's parents. Both children went to college and got professional degrees. By Justine's fiftieth birthday, both of them had moved from Clover Hill permanently. Herman continued to work at the bank."

"Have you located either of the children?"

"I spoke with both of them. Helen should arrive tomorrow and Jacob on Wednesday. Helen shared that Justine and Herman visited her a few times in Seattle — right after the birth of each of the grandchildren. Jacob said the same. He lives in Atlanta. Both indicated they'd occasionally come back to Clover Hill, but hadn't been back since Herman retired."

He shook his head. "They said they were too busy with their jobs and kids. Helen said she called every couple of weeks and talked to Justine less than a month ago. Justine told her Herman was sleeping."

"But how did Justine and Herman function?"

"Ahhh. Apparently, the beauty of technology. When Herman retired, Helen helped them file the paperwork for his pension and social security with direct deposit. She also set up autopay for all the utilities, taxes, Herman's credit card, and any other recurring expenses. Herman used his credit card for groceries and whatever else they needed. Helen was certain he also kept cash somewhere in the house to pay a housekeeper and a young man to help with the yard."

"And we know Dan was the most recent of the young men?"

"Right. He said he's been doing the odd jobs around the house for two years now. He gave me the name of the person who did it before him, all through high school. The school counselor passed on the information to Dan when the other person was about to graduate and leave Clover Hill."

"What about the housekeeper?"

"Helen didn't have any information – and she was a lot more talkative than Jacob. Dan only remembers seeing Herman once, a long time ago. Described him as 'crotchety' and he didn't question where he was. Usually, he only saw Justine."

"All very odd. Did the daughter know about the dogs?"

"No, she was surprised when I asked if Justine mentioned getting a dog. Sounded like Herman wouldn't allow dogs or cats. She doesn't know about the condition of the house, either."

"Oh, my. She is in for a surprise from what I've heard."

"That's for sure. I think they plan on staying there. I asked her to meet me at the station before going to the house – I told her it was still a crime scene."

"That's probably a good idea."

"Sheridan, it might be good if there was a woman available when I meet with her and take her to the house. Would you be willing? Maybe you could explain the hoarding thing."

His request surprised me, yet it also intrigued me. "I should be able to help out. Just let me know when and where."

"Good. With all that, Sheridan, what questions come to mind?"

"For starters, Atlanta is a lot closer to Virginia than Seattle, so why is Helen getting here first?" He shrugged and shook his head.

"Okay, we'll let that go. What happens to the property? Who benefits from Justine's death – regardless of whether or not they knew Herman was deceased already?"

"We haven't located a will as yet, so the estate will go to probate and likely to Helen and Jacob unless someone else comes forward."

"Is there any record of someone who wanted to buy up the land? Anyone checking on the deed or who owns it? Maybe someone who wants the land to put up new condos and figures the heirs will surely want to unload it?"

He leaned back and scratched his head. "I hadn't thought of that possibility. Definitely something to look into. Thanks."

He stood to leave. "I checked by the way. One of those email addresses is Lacie's at the station. Best guess is the other is a personal account. I have someone doing a complete scan of all her emails and phone calls at the station. How many hits did you get on the rest of the rescues?"

"A lot. I think we may have some place for most of them. I'm going to Pets and Paws in a little while to figure out which ones and how many are left."

He nodded. We walked to the door and he stopped. "Did you hear they found four or five more dogs at the edge of the property hunkered down in a shack. Dr. Barksdale has them now."

I shook my head. "We're due for another freeze. I hope there aren't more out there."

He nodded and left. A glance at my watch, and I realized the course would have to wait until after I worked with Mrs. Chantilly to get more dogs to a new location. With the start of school, she'd lost Luke and many of the other volunteers.

CHAPTER 13

Chaos was in full play at Pets and Paws when I arrived. I opened the door and was greeted by three puppies, who all tried to escape. The good news was they were now healthy enough to run around. The bad news, they were running around.

I yelled for Mrs. Chantilly and didn't get a response. Collecting the puppies, I deposited them where they belonged and grabbed the baby gate in the hall to keep them contained.

Barking got my attention and I hustled over to the other area. Not a great idea – all the dogs greeted me loudly. I spotted two more puppies amidst the crates and moved them to the other room.

A quick peek into the last room and it was obvious that no one was watching the dogs in the house. That left the garage, where I found Mrs. Chantilly.

"Oh, Sheridan. I'm so glad you're here. Cocoa died you know. Lacie was so attached to her. Now, she won't get another dog. And that Glenn Peabody, does he care? No, he still won't let her go back to work. So what if some of her sweaters were found in the house. I give clothes to Goodwill all the time. I guess if Justine had been the same size as me, I'd be a suspect."

I blinked, confused. Lacie was nowhere in sight. "Hi, Mrs. Chantilly. Is anyone helping you out today? I understand if Lacie's dog died, she might not want to be here."

"Oh, that was a long time ago, don't you know? I think she's running errands. Yes, that must be it. I got a call from someone, Francie or Marcy or something like that. Anyway Paisley and Plaid are with a foster. The same folks took a few others, too. I made notes of where they went on the clipboards. Now we have fewer dogs down here."

"I have great news. I think I found places for a few more. Let me just check and see which ones have been picked up already. Hopefully, with all the rescues coming forward, the remaining dogs could be moved to the house? How many do you think there's room for up there?"

"What a great idea. I don't think Luke or Susie are coming in until later. I should get back to the house. You let me know if you need anything, okay?"

She turned around and scurried away. I checked the clipboards and from the times noted I figured out that Luke had been there before school. I confirmed with the rescues there were homes for four more of the dogs and marked their clipboards with the information on who was coming to get them and when. I checked food and water and did quick walks with each of the dogs.

My goal before leaving was to get some answers and help Mrs. Chantilly figure out next steps. I only had an hour before I needed to pick up Maddie from school. I heard voices as I approached the front door – one of which I recognized as belonging to Blake Buchanan, the other Mrs. Chantilly.

"Dora, you need to listen. The police are still combing through everything. If Lacie is responsible, she will have to face the consequences. You may not be able to protect her."

"So, they found a few sweaters with Lacie's name on them. She explained she routinely donated clothes when she'd outgrow them. I was always on her about her up and down weight, not eating right, not getting enough exercise."

"Listen to yourself. When was the last time you had a heart to heart with her before this whole mess."

"Well, it seems like yesterday. I'm going to go lie down. I'm not feeling well."

"Dora…"

And then silence. I decided now was as good a time as any to open the door and collided with Blake.

"Sorry, so sorry. I wasn't looking where I was going. Are you all right?"

"Yes, Mr. Buchanan, I'm fine. Do you know if Mrs. Chantilly figured out if there was room to move the dogs from the garage to the house?"

He blinked a few times before he answered. "I don't know. As long as I'm here, why don't we do a walk through. I'm sure she'll be back down in a few minutes. She went to … uh…freshen up."

He nodded and turned around. We stopped where the crates with the original residents were. "Hmm. Do you think we could fit one more in here?

I can check with Dr. Barksdale about it if there's room."

He straightened the crates a bit on one side and then the other. While he did that, I checked all their clipboards and greeted each of them. I'd need to do more than that before I left unless Susie or Luke showed up.

"I think maybe two. Let's check the other rooms."

At the mamas and pups, I dropped some not so subtle hints. "What we need in here are four very large crates or partitions. A few of these puppies are rambunctious and the mamas aren't quite up to the job yet."

He nodded and laughed as one puppy tried to escape through the opening in the baby gate. "Or at least a better baby gate."

The last area on the other side only had six smaller dogs, some of them older puppies. There was possibly enough room for eight more. Once the four were picked up, maybe Luke could move the remaining dogs inside.

"Sheridan, have you seen Lacie today by any chance?"

If not for the conversation I'd overhead, I wouldn't have thought anything of it. I answered cautiously, "Mrs. Chantilly said something about her dog dying?"

He exhaled and looked away, as if lost in thought.

"That was a long time ago. Lacie's dog died in her arms when she was 12. She blamed her parents – she'd told them the dog was sick and needed to see the vet. Her father was a drunk and gambled away all their money. He didn't care about Lacie or the dog and just tossed the dog in the trash. Then he told Lacie she'd better be careful or she'd join the dog."

He shook his head. "She ... she became quite a problem at home, in the community, and at school. I always believed it was so someone would take her out of that house. It's hard to see the scars left by emotional abuse. It took a year and then some time in juvie before she moved in here with Dora."

"And she ended up working for the police? That's impressive. I'd count that as a positive outcome."

"I hope you're right, Sheridan. Unfortunately, there's a lot of circumstantial evidence right now and all of it points to Lacie."

We both turned as we heard Luke's "hello." Inasmuch as Mrs. Chantilly hadn't come back down, I gave him the information on the rescues and fosters. I also shared that it looked like when the next batch were picked up, the others would fit, albeit in close quarters, in the house. That would at least make keeping track of them easier.

At home, I grabbed the mail and sorted through the after holidays sales, the January sales, the early Valentine's sales, a few bills, and an envelope with no return address and a typed address label with my name misspelled.

I was about to presume it was somebody wanting money when I realized it had no stamp. It had been placed in the mail box by somebody, not the mail person. I opened it up and almost laughed out loud. Someone had created an electronic version of the letters people might get in the old mysteries I loved to read with words cut out from other places and pasted together – only electronically with "cut and paste."

The message was simple. "Mind your own business lady." I carefully set it down, with the envelope, out of the way of my food preparation. When Brett got home, I shared the letter with him. He shook his head and used tongs to put both in a plastic bag. Maybe the person left fingerprints. Although there were no threats, whoever had left it knew where we lived.

CHAPTER 14

I poured myself a cup of coffee, my wake-up fix. Brett cleared his throat. "I'm glad you've helped Mrs. Chantilly get the dogs all squared away, but until this murder is solved and Lacie exonerated, I'd feel better if you weren't involved in the investigation itself."

I bristled at this recurring theme. "I'm not 'involved' in the investigation, Brett. I'm only helping the Chief with his meeting so there's someone there if she gets upset. My only 'investigation' has been to figure out where all the dogs came from. As for Lacie, I barely talk to her except about the care of the dogs in the garage. The only information she shared was for me to mind my own business."

He groaned. "What is your take on her? As a psychologist? Do you think she's the one who sent the letter?"

I tried not to smile. He always wanted me not involved and then asked my opinion. "Blake told me she was emotionally abused by an alcoholic father, rebelled, and that's how she ended up with Mrs.

Chantilly. From what I've seen, she's withdrawn and doesn't choose to interact with people beyond what's absolutely necessary. Definite trust and betrayal issues. I guess that works as a dispatcher – just the facts, no small talk. On the other hand, she's ... Willie called her a 'dog whisperer' and that fits. She communes with the dogs, calms them, and they respond to her."

"You get along with the dogs. So does Nedra. How is she different?"

I glanced away and tried to find the words to explain it. "These dogs. All abandoned. She'd talk softly and they'd stop whining or howling or growling. It was as if she soothed their pain, their suffering, and their fears, one at a time, effortlessly. Nedra and I? We loved on them, cleaned their cages and made friends, but it wasn't the same 'peace' she gives them in an instant, and we didn't always know what the problem was. She did. They spoke and she heard what they said."

"Could she get them to act on her behalf? You know, prompt them to attack someone?"

I cringed at the thought. "They didn't act protective of her or react when any other dog growled at her."

I hesitated, knowing I hadn't answered his question. "I suspect she is capable of training them to attack or herd or anything else. And then, yes, they would respond to her prompt. Of that I am sure."

He scowled and glanced at his watch. "Time to go. Stay safe and remember the daughter and son aren't just victims, they're possible suspects."

He cut my eye roll short with a quick kiss goodbye. Maddie bolted out of her room and with a quick "I'm late" disappeared out the door. Thankfully, she managed to catch the bus. I cleaned up and then headed to the station to meet the Chief and Justine's daughter.

At the station, I noticed a woman about my age sitting on a bench. She had reddish brown hair, cropped, and wore glasses with dark rims. She had a heavy coat and boots. Nice boots. Engrossed with her phone, she didn't seem to notice I was studying her. She shook her head at whatever she read and her shoulders slumped.

I checked with reception and was advised the chief would be with us promptly now that I arrived. I toyed with the idea of introducing myself but decided to let the chief explain my presence. It would be better coming from him. I no sooner sat down and the door to the back opened and Chief Peabody appeared.

"Mrs. Wharton?" The woman nodded and stood. "I'm Chief Peabody. Thank you for meeting with me. I've asked Sheridan Hendley to sit in as she may be able to help in some way."

I joined them as he said my name. At her puzzled expression, I offered, "Glad to be of help, Mrs. Wharton. I'm a psychologist though mostly I teach at a local college. I also volunteer with the local dog shelter." She nodded but her tight lips indicated she wasn't thrilled.

"I have coffee set up in the conference room. Shall we?"

I nodded and followed behind Mrs. Wharton to the conference room, which was not too fancy and not too shabby. I immediately zeroed in on the coffee pot. To feel useful, I played hostess and poured everyone coffee. Once we were settled, Chief Peabody cleared his throat.

"Mrs. Wharton, this is an informal meeting, however, I'd like to record the interview. My note-taking skills are not all that great. Is that agreeable with you?"

She nodded. He turned on the recorder and provided the date and identified the three of us before beginning. He scribbled something on his notepad as well.

"Mrs. Wharton, as I explained on the phone, earlier this past week your mother, Justine Stoneham, was found, deceased, at the family home. Subsequently, we located the grave for your father, Herman Stoneham, in the backyard."

"How? What happened? I'm having a hard time understanding this."

The chief started at her questions, his face showing his surprise. "As I explained, as best as the coroner could determine, your father died of natural causes, approximately twelve months ago, maybe as many as eighteen. This is consistent with the last time anyone actually saw him or talked to him as far as we can determine."

"That can't be right. I spoke to my mother just a few weeks ago. I called at least once a month to check on them."

The chief leaned forward. "And when was the last time you actually spoke to your father?"

Her blue eyes widened and her jaw dropped. "I… I don't know. Usually I talked to mom and she would tell me everything was fine. Dad was in the garden or went for a walk or was taking a nap." She paused.

"You're telling me he was dead all that time for the last year or more and she didn't tell me or Jacob?" Her voice rose and I shifted closer to pat her arm.

"Yes, ma'am. I'm afraid so. Neither of them ever came to town or socialized other than church and Pastor Pete said he hasn't seen them in over a year. Raises a lot of questions about how they functioned."

She nodded and sat up straighter. "I think I explained some of that when we spoke on the phone. Jacob and I left Clover Hill for college and both of us pretty much left for good. We'd both come home for holidays – at least until we had kids and travel was more difficult. Dad took care of everything and though I tried to convince them Mom needed to have her own credit card and at least be listed on everything, Dad was pretty old school." She grimaced and shook her head.

"You indicated everything was electronic when we spoke."

"Yes, sir. When Dad retired from the bank, we – Jacob and I – sat down with them and I set everything for autodeposit and autopay. My Dad was a little old-fashioned and he wanted some cash on hand at the house. He had a debit card so he could always go to the bank or most stores and get more cash if he needed it."

"Any idea what he would need cash for?"

"Oh, yeah. When we first moved out, they hired some woman to help with housekeeping and paid her in cash." She put her hands up. "I know that's technically not legal, but the woman was local – not an immigrant – and life was simpler back then. When Dad retired, it was some girl who came out once a month to help with housekeeping. I think it was the daughter of the woman they'd hired to begin with. And then the young man who helped with the landscaping."

"Do you know any of their names? That could be helpful."

"No. Sorry, I can't remember their names. The Pastor may know though if it's still the same one. He's the one who found the first woman, asked my dad to help her out as she was in a bad situation or something. I don't know about the younger one. My mom mentioned she'd been in trouble as a teen. I only met her once and I didn't quite trust her."

"Do you remember what she looked like? Why you didn't trust her?"

"Not what she looked like. I think she was in high school or just graduated? She just wasn't very friendly and knowing she'd been in trouble before…"

"You haven't been back to see them since Herman retired?"

"No, and now I regret that. They came to visit when our kids were born and once or twice, and otherwise I tried to keep in touch. I used to talk to them more often. Lately, only about once a month. Stan, my ex-husband, and I bought them smart phones, but they wouldn't use them. They didn't have an answering machine and they liked to sit outside, work in the garden, and go for walks. Most times, I'd have to try calling three or four times before someone answered."

"Can you describe what the house looked like when you were last there?"

"Neat, clean, everything in its place. Now, the housekeeper had just been there to get the place ready for us. I don't suppose you know who the current housekeeper is or had her get our rooms ready. Jacob will arrive tomorrow."

CHAPTER 15

I cleared my throat and Mrs. Wharton turned to me, eyebrows raised. "Were either of your parents collectors – you know, like figurines or china?"

She sat up straight. "Not at all. The house is very small by today's standards. Three bedrooms upstairs, but they are on the small size. Even the master couldn't accommodate more than a full-size bed. Kitchen, dining room and living room downstairs weren't all that big. No place to store or show off anything like that. Why do you ask?"

I looked to the chief and he exhaled. "Mrs. Wharton. There's no easy way to describe the house right now. It doesn't look like your parents threw away anything for the past several years. And they had items shipped to the house."

She shook her head and I continued. "When the police arrived at the house? They had trouble even walking through the house. Boxes and papers and mail stacked everywhere. Definitely, no housekeeper."

Mrs. Wharton glanced from the chief to me. "I... I don't understand." I put my hand on her arm.

"It sounds like your parents – or at least your mother – kept things, collected things, hoarded things to fill a vacuum or feel like she or they mattered. Dogs, too."

"No, my father wouldn't have allowed dogs. If you found a dog there, it wandered from some place nearby."

"I'm sorry. Your mother adopted several dogs from rescues over the past year. She told one of them she wanted a dog because she was lonely after her husband died. I've been in contact with multiple rescues and they all told the same story."

She was silent for a minute. "No. This is crazy." She stood up. "I'm going to the house now. You must be mistaken."

The chief and I stood as well. "Sheridan and I will follow you. It is still a crime scene." We all walked out together and I accepted the chief's offer to ride with him as long as it was in the front seat.

"What do you think?"

"Not a very close family and she is in for a shock. Did you ever find the cash she indicated Mr. Stoneham kept on hand? Somehow she paid Dan in October."

"Not yet. No telling where she stashed it. Oh, and by the way, some more packages arrived. Apparently the shipments are automatic. Mrs. Wharton will have to deal with those and returns."

"That will be the easiest thing she has to deal with."

He nodded. "She's speeding, but I guess she's in panic mode. I don't have the heart to give her a ticket knowing what she's about to face."

Soon enough, we turned down a dirt road. Mrs. Wharton stopped at the mail box, a package sitting on top of it. She looked at us as she picked up the package and took the mail. Her grimace and knit brows indicated confusion on her part and something more negative, perhaps anger that mail and packages were still being delivered.

It was as Brett described. There was no way the mailperson or delivery person could see the house from the mailbox. We followed her up the driveway and through trees until we reached the house. A policeman saluted us.

The house looked bigger than I expected given her description. A two-story home with a wraparound porch. It was old and needed a good painting and some repairs to the porch that I could see. She stood staring at the house and we joined her. She glared at the chief as if he was responsible for the condition.

"I thought someone came to help with repairs and the yard?"

"A young man named Dan mowed the lawn and cleared away dead branches and such. He was last here in October and due to come back in March."

"Has it changed much since you were last here?"

She looked at me before she answered. "It looks older. The chairs on the deck. Where'd they go. It needs some work for sure." She took a deep breath. "Why are there boxes and paper and I don't know what on the porch?"

"In order to get inside and get the stretcher in and out, we had to move some of the boxes out of the way. We didn't want to destroy or remove anything."

"That's ridiculous!" She started up the short stairs and we followed behind her. She fiddled in her purse, then stopped, shaking her head. "Key?"

The chief responded, "Door's open. It was open when we got here."

"Now that's irresponsible. Someone could have come in and burglarized the place. Have you no concern for my parents' belongings? What kind of police are you? Is this because of that silly feud with the Buchanans?"

Chief Peabody took a step back. "Ma'am, begging your pardon. I've had an officer here round the clock. We don't have a key and we are still investigating a crime."

She opened the door and lifted her foot as if she were going to stomp right in. Only she screeched and lost her balance. The chief caught her and I got my first view and whiff of the house. There were boxes or stacks of papers at least four feet high for as long as I could see. I knew from the early descriptions, the overflow on the porch created a wide path at least part way into the house. The chief managed to shift Mrs. Wharton so that she could sit on one of the boxes that offended her so much.

"I... I... where did all this come from? What is that smell?"

"Mrs. Wharton, that's what I was trying to explain back at the station. At some point, your parents or more likely your mother, started saving everything and anything. If your dad liked things neat, she probably started in the rooms not being used or seen."

"My room and Jacob's."

I nodded.

"The smell is because when she adopted dogs, apparently some of them stayed inside and were still inside when the police arrived."

"What? Wait. How were they inside? These stacks are only here?" She stood up.

"No, ma'am. They're everywhere with paths like a maze. We found the dogs going through the maze and with the help of another dog. Some weren't able to get out."

She sat back down, shoulders slumped and head in her hands.

"Ma'am, I took the liberty of making reservations for you and for your brother at the Sleep Softly Inn in town. Staying here is not an option. If you'd like, we can walk through with you. We have no idea what might be of value in here – financially or otherwise. We can arrange for a dumpster and probably find some strong boys to help clean this up, but you and your brother will have to figure out what can be tossed and what can't."

"Walk through first. Then I'll call Jacob. You found my parents in here? How?"

"We found Justine inside the house. We could hear dogs yelping or barking and made our way to them to get them out, assuming the place was abandoned. Justine was in one of the bedrooms upstairs. The next day we had two dogs checking outside. Your dad was buried in a shallow grave in the backyard. I'm sorry."

She nodded and stood, shoulders slumped and hands trembling. "Let's get this over with and then you can show me the backyard."

CHAPTER 16

We walked in. I left the door open to let in some air and light. We followed the larger path and the chief pointed out narrower paths on either side. Only a narrow sliver of windows was visible, letting in only minimum light.

I wanted to turn on lights but didn't see any switches. I noticed some stacks high and some lower, with no dust on the low ones. Stacks had been moved, probably to gain access.

The wider path ended at the stairs, which were remarkably clear. Probably necessary to get Justine's body out of the house. A quick few steps into the kitchen and a narrow path that paralleled the counter, sink, stove and refrigerator. The back door was hidden – if the house had gone up in flames there'd have been only one way out.

Upstairs, the smell was worse. The hallway was only cleared on the short end. Justine's room. Mrs. Wharton gasped and leaned against the wall of boxes.

"The smell. Can't we open some windows or something? Is the heat on?"

"If we could get to them, we could, only then if it rains…" He shrugged.

"We ordered the heat to be turned off. This…" He waved his arms, "…is a major fire hazard. Lucky the place didn't burn down."

She nodded and stepped toward the master bedroom. She pushed the door as far open as it could get and gasped again. The chief caught her as she fainted.

He motioned for me to close the door, which I did. I caught a glimpse in the process and understood her reaction. Nothing had been cleaned up after Justine's death.

The chief stayed with her and I ventured to the other end, a tight squeeze for my size ten body. I could only open the other three doors enough to identify them. A bathroom which had the most open space, a pink room, and a blue room. I walked back as Mrs. Wharton regained her strength.

"The doors to the other rooms only open part way. The bathroom is the most accessible. I'm not sure that tells you much."

She shook her head. "This is unbelievable. I have to take a picture even if it feels ghoulish. Jacob won't believe me without a picture. He'll be very angry."

She pulled out her phone and took a picture of the hall. We went back downstairs. She took one of the kitchen and one of the main living area. Then she headed for the door.

"Mrs. Wharton, before we leave the house, at least as of October, Justine still had cash on hand to pay Dan when he mowed. Do you have any idea where she might have kept it? With no idea how much money we are talking about, I'd be more comfortable if we could find it and account for it."

Her mouth dropped. "I don't know." She looked around at the many boxes and threw her hands up in the air.

"You're right. It could be in any one of these boxes or stacks. Chief, have you eliminated the most accessible places?"

"Like where?"

"The kitchen. On the counter? In the cabinets or drawers? In the dishwasher? The oven? The fridge?" I suggested.

He turned around and we followed. "Mrs. Wharton, will you do the honors and check out the places Sheridan mentioned?"

We all trudged back to the kitchen. I found a light switch and ceiling lights added some light – and shadows. Eerie. Mrs. Wharton's attempt to walk down the path was thwarted by her heavy winter coat.

"I'd have to take my coat off and it's too cold." She backed up.

"Sheridan? I certainly won't fit."

I squeezed my way to the far end and the fridge. I opened the door and stepped back as far as I could. Someone needed to clean it out, but nothing that looked like it might contain money. I checked the freezer and no unidentified packages there. The oven was empty and I reached up and opened cabinets over the stove and the sink. Dishwasher was full. I pulled out the first drawer – the junk drawer in our kitchen – and held up a manila envelope. I scooted down to Mrs. Wharton and handed it to her.

She opened it and pulled out what looked like a listing of what was paid and to whom and money. Lots of money.

"Please count the money and then I'll have Sheridan re-count it. We'll mark it on the envelope. I'm afraid the money and the papers will become evidence."

"I'm sorry. I missed something somewhere. Evidence of what?"

"Your mother's death has been ruled "suspicious" and whom she was paying and for what could lead us to the murderer."

"Why suspicious and not natural causes like my dad?"

"There's evidence Justine sustained a head injury, while there was no indication of foul play with your dad."

She nodded. "Who would kill her? Why? Couldn't she have fallen and hit her head on something?"

"That's the part that's not clear. The coroner can't reach a conclusion without more information. In the meantime, this is an open investigation into a suspicious death."

We both counted the money, indicated the amount on the envelope and he took possession. A quick trip to the backyard and we stopped at the cars.

"Mrs. Wharton, do you know if anyone contacted your parents about selling the property? Or perhaps contacted you or Jacob?"

She snorted. "The only ones I ever heard wanted to buy the property were the Buchanans. And that was years ago. My dad mentioned some realtor once, surprised at the appraisal value, but he didn't talk about selling to me. I'll check with Jacob."

"Sleep Softly Inn, you said?" At the chief's nod, she added, "I guess you know where I'll be until Jacob gets here."

"Yes, ma'am. When he gets here, please let me know. I'll need to get some signatures for us to review bank records. Do you happen to know who has Power of Attorney or has a copy of your parents' wills?"

She huffed. "Jacob, I suspect. Dad didn't think women should be involved in finance or legal stuff. Hence, mom had access to accounts without actually owning anything herself."

CHAPTER 17

At home, I immediately showered, cuddled Charlie and Bella, and then walked through the house. A quick glance into the garage and the unpacked boxes from my move, and I shuddered. I sat down with a cup of coffee and my phone chirped.

"Hi, Chief."

"Sheridan. Thank you for helping out today. Did anything come to mind since we chatted on the way to the house?"

"She was stunned by the condition of the house – she isn't the killer, though I guess she could have arranged for it to happen thinking the house was worth a lot."

"I agree. Anything else?"

"She hadn't processed the suspicious death part at all. Also there's some tension between Helen and Jacob. Did you get anything useful from the papers in the envelope?"

"Yes. All I am willing to share is that I now know who the housekeepers were prior to Herman's retirement and a few years thereafter. No housekeeper was paid for the past eighteen months."

"That would be after Herman died then?"

"Timing would be right. I hate to ask this Sheridan, but can you spare a couple of hours tomorrow? After Jacob arrives? I'd like your take on him and his reactions."

I hesitated. My syllabi and class activities still waited. Curiosity got the better of me though. "Sure. What time shall I plan on meeting you and where?"

"I'll give you a call around two o'clock and let you know the details."

We disconnected as Maddie got home. She was smiling and that was always a good sign. "How'd your day go?"

"Okay. Mr. Simpson talked about the spring concert. Auditions for the solos are next Monday. I want to decide which ones I want to try for."

"That's quick. Maybe over the weekend you could try singing all the songs and 'audition' for your dad and me. How's that sound?"

"Great. There're only four songs so it won't take long. How are the dogs at Pets and Paws? I'm worried about them."

"Almost all are back in foster care. A lot less crazy there, I think. We'll go check on them on Saturday. In the meantime, you get your homework done and I'll get dinner.

I ruminated over the Stoneham house and the stuff stacked as I sorted through pots and pans and the ever exploding collection of plastic containers. As the meat cooked, I sat on the floor and matched containers with tops. Sure enough, I ended with some containers with no tops and some tops with missing containers. I shoved them in a bag for Goodwill. Brett arrived as I closed the bag up.

"What do you have there?" He pointed to the bag.

"Those are plastic containers that have no lids and lids with no containers. Goodwill."

"Hey, maybe I could use some of those in the garage."

I shuddered and shook my head. "After seeing the Stoneham house, I ... we have to get rid of stuff that's not worth saving. It will just accumulate and grow ...all those boxes in the garage."

He took me in his arms and chuckled. "It's okay. I don't think a few odd containers will ever reach that level. As for the boxes, my life rule has been if a box hasn't needed to be opened in a few years – other than tax and legal documents and photographs – then I probably don't need anything in that box. Those boxes have only been there for about six months and you've needed to get to them since then."

"Okay, you're right. As long as we keep it under control. Max used to boast he still had his report cards from first grade through college. He said he liked to look through them to remind himself how smart he was."

"You mean I have to throw mine away?" His mouth twitched.

"You don't really?"

He laughed. "No, but I do have some of Maddie's and I wouldn't be surprised if my mother didn't save all our report cards."

"Hmm. I guess that's true. I don't know what we'll ever find when the time comes with either of our parents. At least we know we can walk through the house and sit on furniture and see out the windows…"

He hugged me again. "That bad, huh?"

"Yes. And, it may seem morbid, and I know both our parents are healthy, but do you know where your parents keep their will or who has Power of Attorney or any of that? I sure don't."

"I have a copy of their wills and each has Power of Attorney for the other, and I'm the back up. Maybe you could check with your parents? Or with Kaylie or Kevin?"

"I'll ask my mother when I talk to her on Sunday."

"That reminds me though, my will needs to be revised. Do you have one?"

I shrugged. "Everything in banks and retirement has beneficiaries. That only left the house and car."

"I'll make an appointment with my attorney and we'll both go and get that taken care of. In the meantime, I'm starved. And later I want to hear what happened with the daughter."

Together, we got dinner on the table and Maddie wandered in singing a song I didn't recognize. Bella and Charlie following her. Once Maddie retired to her room, Bella with her, Brett cleared his throat.

"There were no fingerprints on the letter or envelope other than yours. Other than Lacie, anyone else tell you to mind your business lately?"

"No, and even Lacie? She's only seen me at Pets and Paws. How would she know where I live? I checked and even if they did an online search, they'd get my address in Cold Creek, the College address there, or the Millicent College address in Lynchburg. How would she have gotten this address?"

He shook his head. "No idea. But think about it. Would she ever have access to your purse, your driver's license?"

"I guess she could have gone through my purse at Pets and Paws, still that would be risky with all the people there the past two weeks."

"Well, that's one possibility. Do you always lock your car or could she have pulled your registration?"

My face fell. "I don't always remember, so yes that's possible. Again, with Blake and everyone coming and going?"

"At least there was no threat, but this is the second time. Be sure to lock your doors from here on out." He shrugged his shoulders. "So, what did you think of the daughter? Is she a viable suspect?"

I shook my head. "She was too shocked at the condition of the house for one. Justine was upstairs and the pathway had to be enlarged by the police to get up there. Helen is bigger than I am and she didn't fit in the paths that hadn't been widened. That means she physically couldn't have killed Justine upstairs."

"I wonder. Is it possible someone hit her in one place and she crawled upstairs to die."

"I don't know. I've heard of that happening with head injuries. If that were possible, then Helen could have done it and faked her shock. We did find the stash of cash she used to pay Dan. A little over a thousand dollars, all in twenties. Like it came from an ATM."

"Where was it hidden?"

I chuckled. "Not exactly hidden. Stashed in a drawer in the kitchen in a manila envelope. More like her 'mad money' in a convenient place. The chief has it now."

"What next?"

"Tomorrow, Jacob arrives and I'm joining the party to see his reactions.

CHAPTER 18

Before the call from the chief, I managed to nail down my syllabi for the courses I'd be teaching and create the online shell for students. His call provided the perfect excuse for a much needed break from the tedious part of an academic position.

I dressed and arrived at the station in plenty of time, hoping to talk with him before Helen and Jacob arrived. No such luck.

"What do you mean you don't know what happened yet? What kind of imbeciles are you anyway? Nothing has changed in twenty years." The man was standing very close to Chief Peabody, his hands fisted. He was as tall as the chief and stocky. The chief's face was red and the one other officer had moved closer. Helen cowered behind her brother.

"Mr. Stoneham, I realize you are in shock. Neither of your parents contacted the police or anyone else we know of to ask for assistance at any point. We didn't know there were any problems. Bills were being paid, mail collected, packages delivered.

Up until three months ago, your mother was paying someone to mow the lawn."

"How could they accumulate fifty dogs without anyone noticing? Never mind the wasted money. Didn't anyone notice she was buying dog food? The vet? Unbelievable!"

The chief cleared his throat. "We haven't figured out all the details. However, the local veterinarian never even met your mother or father. Justine didn't take any of the dogs to her. There were no vet bills."

"And Helen here must have misunderstood. She said my father died over a year ago? How was that kept a secret? My word. I could've sold that property already." He took a step back. "Helen obviously exaggerated the condition of the house, not that it matters. All JJ Properties wanted was the land anyway. Let's go."

He turned and marched away, only stopping long enough to grab Helen's arm and propel her along with him. I moved out of the way lest he run me over.

The chief shook his head. "Thanks for coming, Sheridan. Give them a few minutes – he can do to cool his heels. And if he's speeding? Him, I'll ticket."

A few minutes later and we were on our way, just under the speed limit. I took advantage of the time.

"Did I miss anything?"

"Let's see, you walked in about when it was all our fault, right?" He chuckled.

"Yeah, and he was angry."

"Ahh. You missed the good part, then. All else aside, he's angry because there is no will. The property has always been passed from father to son, at least as far as he's concerned. In his mind, it should have immediately become his when Herman died. I clarified the law generally with the caveat he'd need to verify with an attorney. Virginia doesn't have community property rights per se but in the event of one spouse's death, if the property will be used by the surviving spouse, I think it would be considered hers under marital rights."

He shrugged. "I emphasized that he needed to get an attorney as without a will, the estate would go to probate, and under marital rights, the property likely belonged to Justine. I made the 'mistake' of suggesting the estate might be split between Helen and him. He glowered at her and then exploded at me."

"I didn't realize that about Virginia law. I've half a mind to directly suggest Helen get an attorney to fight for her share." As I thought about it, I realized that might explain why Brett's ex, Victoria, got their house when they divorced.

We turned to go up the driveway. "Before I forget, have you ever heard of JJ Properties?"

He shook his head. As we pulled up to the house, he slammed on his brakes and bolted out of the car. I followed. Helen was on the ground sobbing with Jacob standing over her screaming.

"You did this. You always resented that I'd get the house and all this property – the only thing of real value here. Couldn't you keep track of them? There may be nothing left in his accounts. Did you ever consider that? I counted on that money for my son's college fund."

Chief Peabody moved between Jacob and Helen and I knelt by her side.

"No use, like most women. And you probably blame me for your disaster of a marriage. He left you for some rich broad once he realized you wouldn't ever inherit."

"Mr. Stoneham, I'm going to ask you nicely to back up here."

Jacob shook his head as if in realization the Chief blocked Helen at that point. "This is none of your business. Stay out of it."

"I can't do that, sir. We have a suspicious death here and I'm not sure what else. Let's go inside so you can see for yourself."

The chief took a step forward, prompting Jacob to step backward and they walked into the house.

"Helen, are you okay? Are you injured?"

She nodded yes to the first and no to the second. She tried to sit up and I helped her.

"Can you tell me how you ended up on the ground here?"

"I... He pushed me. He was yelling at me that it was all my fault and pushed me. I'm okay."

"When was the last time you and Jacob got together?"

"When my father retired. He reminded me that this would all be his to do with as he wanted some day. All I heard all my life was the father-to-son litany. And something about it being law. Is that even possible?"

I shrugged. "I'm not a lawyer so I don't know. I'd suggest you get yourself an estate attorney here in Virginia to act on your behalf. In the meantime, let's get you standing up."

I helped her up as the men exited the house. Jacob opened his mouth to speak and I intervened.

"Mr. Stoneham, I don't believe we've been introduced. I'm Sheridan Hendley." With my boots on I was only a few inches shorter than he was and I looked him in the eyes.

"Dr. Hendley assists the police here and elsewhere with murder investigations."

Jacob looked from the chief to me, then back to the chief.

"Mr. Stoneham, I realize Chief Peabody may have already asked this, but when did you last speak with your father or mother? Visit last?"

"We weren't exactly a close family. The only 'tie' that bound any of the Stonehams is this land. Last time I was here was the retirement party. I oversaw as Helen took care of setting everything up electronically for our father. Look where that got us." He glared at her and she would have stepped back if not for my arm behind her.

"It's unfortunate that you weren't closer to your parents. Maybe then you'd have been suspicious or more aware of what happened."

His fists clenched again. "You've no right to say those things. None at all. Just mind your own business, you hear."

I nodded but held my ground. The chief cleared his throat.

"It is probably an insurmountable task to look through all the stacks in there. However, if there is any legal document as you suggested or a will, that needs to be found. Without any documentation, I will notify the appropriate authorities to take control until the estate can be probated."

"Helen, when you set up everything with the bank, did you designate someone with authority to sign off or anything?"

"I... I don't remember. I know both Herman and I signed a lot of papers."

I controlled my urge to do a fist pump and cheer. I glanced at the chief and could tell he was trying not to smile as he directed his next comments.

"The bank might be the place to start then, Helen. The coroner can provide you with the death certificate for your father. You also need to make arrangements for burial and any memorial services you might want. Once you pick up the death certificate, since everything is in your father's name, the bank will take steps to stop the autopays – and perhaps be able to stop the automated delivery of dog food."

"I am the man here. Why are you talking to her?" He turned and glared at the chief.

"My apologies. You indicated she worked with the bank to begin with and she indicated she signed forms there. Of course, either one of you can likely deliver the death certificate and take care of notifying the retirement account and social security."

"She can take care of all that accounting stuff. Only thing she's good for."

Helen started to sob and I pulled her closer. I whispered, "You are going to need an attorney, but you may be okay."

"Do either of you know if he had a safe deposit box or safe anywhere?"

Jacob groaned. "I think there was a small gun safe in one of the closets. He kept a revolver in it. I don't remember which one. Years ago, he had a rifle and it was hung on the wall in the main room."

"As I told Helen yesterday, we can arrange to have a dumpster brought in. How you sift through it is up to you. Without any legal documentation, I will be contacting appropriate persons for probate action. Sheridan, let's go."

I nodded and turned to Helen. "You can reach me through the chief if you need to talk." I nodded to Jacob and we left.

CHAPTER 19

Coming out of the grocery store, I spotted one of our neighbors, Heather, talking to someone by my car. She had her baby in her arms and I smiled until she pointed at my car. And my flat tire.

"Sheridan, you have a flat." She bounced her baby and the man nodded.

I groaned. My new car and its first flat. "It was fine when I went in the store."

"It happens. Better here in the lot than on the road. Hank – Hank Hamilton. I can give you a hand with your spare if you'd like." I'd yet to meet Hank and had to admit, he and Heather made a beautiful couple.

I smiled. "Nice to meet you Hank. That'd be great, only I don't want to hold you guys up."

"No problem. You can talk to Heather and Holly while I take care of it. Keys?"

I shifted my bags and unlocked the doors so I could put my groceries in the back seat. Then I handed him the keys and said hello to Holly.

"She's beautiful." The baby cooed and smiled. "Let me see if I can help Hank in any way."

Between us, mostly Hank, my spare was on the car and I was headed home. Thankfully, I didn't have to drive far and Maddie had a ride home after choir practice. I texted Brett to let him know the tire needed to be repaired. He texted back he'd come by and get the car. He arrived a few minutes later.

"You and your cars." He chuckled. He was right though. Somehow my car took a toll whenever I got involved in a murder. This time though, I wasn't really involved in the murder investigation. At least that's what I told myself.

Brett must have read my mind as he added, "In all likelihood, when you were over at the Stoneham place, you picked up a nail or glass or something. I'll take your car and be back in time for dinner." He gave me a kiss and left me to fix dinner.

I shook my head as he drove away. I'd only been to the Stoneham place in the chief's car, so that isn't where I picked up something. Maybe in the parking lot at Pets and Paws.

Maddie arrived a little later. "Huh? You're here. Where's your car? Is Dad here?"

I explained the flat tire and she shrugged, muttered "Homework," and disappeared down the hall singing "My Favorite Things."

Brett arrived as I was taking dinner out of the oven. I started to smile and caught the scowl on his face. He had opened his mouth to say something when Maddie came into the kitchen.

"Dinner smells good. Is it ready? I'm hungry."

I laughed as I put it on the table with Brett's help. Maddie talked all through dinner about choir and homework woes. As usual, she put her dishes in the sink and darted from the kitchen with the single word "homework."

"Do you think she really has that much homework or does she know we won't say 'homework after you help with clean up?' I wonder sometimes."

"No idea. She gets good grades so she obviously does her homework. But now tell me, who's mad at you this time?"

At my expression, he snorted. "Sheridan, the tire was slashed. If this didn't happen so often, if you hadn't gotten the other notes to mind your business…"

My mouth dropped. "I don't know. I mean I didn't make any friends with Jacob Stoneham today, but how would he even know my car? I rode with the chief."

"Okay, maybe it is a coincidence or the same person. What's the story with Stoneham?"

"Other than he's a bully and a chauvinist pig?" I could tell my voice rose as I spoke.

He chuckled and signaled with his hand for me to lower my voice. "Tell me what you really think, Sher."

"I think he's angry enough about not knowing his dad died that he could have killed Justine. He knocked his sister to the ground at the house."

"Why would it matter when his dad died?"

"I'm not too sure on the legal side of this. He believes that when his father died, the house and land would go to him and he planned to sell it. As far as he was concerned, Justine had no claim on the house. It would go from father to son. Correct or not, that's his

his belief. Where did he think Justine would go? What if there was no son?"

Brett shook his head. "No will? Just 'this is the way it was supposed to be'?"

"No will that any one knows of. If generations inherited father to son, can that be interpreted as legally binding and excluding the wife and sisters?"

"I guess if, at some point, there was a trust fund set up that stipulated it. But that would be filed some place. Maybe there are some old papers in the house that specify it. As long as they're executed and witnessed, and say what he thinks they say, then I guess he would have inherited at the time of Herman's death. Huh."

"He mentioned some company – JJ Properties. He said they wanted to buy the land. And he's prepared to sell."

"Well, that gives him motive. It won't sit well with Blake Buchanan for sure. I guess the courts will have to figure it out."

My phone chirped I muttered, "It's the chief."

"Hello, Chief."

"Hello, Sheridan. Mrs. Wharton called and wanted your number. She and Jacob are going to try to go through boxes and stacks to get to the safe in the downstairs closet. She wanted to see if you could be there with her. I'll be more comfortable if more people are there. And I did arrange for the dumpster. They plan to go to the bank first. Can you make it by noon?"

"Yes, that'll work. I planned to help out at Pets and Paws in the morning. I can go to the Stoneham place right after."

Brett mouthed "Tell him about the tire."

"One more thing, Chief. Someone slashed a tire on my car this afternoon."

"Any witnesses?"

"None that I know of. Brett got it taken care of – the tire is in my trunk."

"Okay. I'll make a note and see you tomorrow."

When I got off the phone, Brett was busily doing something on his phone.

"Okay, my calendar is fairly clear tomorrow. Paperwork can wait and I can be a good citizen and help out over there, too."

CHAPTER 20

When I let Charlie and Bella out, the wind and lower temperature reminded me it really was winter and I dressed accordingly. Brett decided to come with me to Pets and Paws after we finished breakfast and both our dogs were all set. His explanation was that it would be easier for us to go to the Stoneham place together. We arrived and parked. I got out of the car and listened.

"It's a nice day for sure, although a bit chilly. What are you waiting for?"

I laughed. "The last few days when I got here? I could hear the yelling from out here. And the garage is closed and dark. And I don't see Mrs. Chantilly's car. All good signs in my book."

He smiled and we went in. We found Mrs. Chantilly in the kitchen.

"Good morning, Sheridan, Detective. What brings you here today, Detective?"

"Nothing official, Mrs. Chantilly. Sheridan and I have some errands to run after helping out this morning so I came along. How's it going?"

"Organized chaos as usual. Lacie's a good girl and she's helping out. We're a little over capacity here. Of course, an adoption day is the way to go. Do you know Lacie, Detective? She is so good with dogs and technology. Oh, and Dr. Barksdale cleared all the dogs, though she'll check back in especially on Horatio and Ghost – broken legs, you know. Lacie, she still doesn't deal well with death. You'll help her Sheridan, I know you will. Time to make biscuits."

She walked away and I risked looking at Brett for his response to her usual dialogue of sorts. He shook his head. "Interesting to say the least. Is anyone else here helping right now?"

I shrugged. "Luke should be at school. I'm not sure about Lacie. The other volunteers are all back at work so they come in when they aren't working. There's usually a schedule in the kitchen. Let's take a tour and see where help is most needed."

Coffees in hand, we started with the side room with mamas and puppies. The room was relatively quiet and only the mamas' heads could be seen above short barriers around each group, four in all. I smiled.

"What's the smile for?"

"I mentioned to Blake the need for some way to partition the mamas to keep the pups with the mama – either large enough crates or some kind of walls. Magically, they're here. And just the right size for mama to see out and to be able to get the pups out as needed or keep the pups inside." I tilted my head. "They remind me of baby play pens."

"Maybe that's what they were to begin with."

I nodded. "Let me check the clipboards. Can you walk around and get a head count of puppies?"

That information was on the clipboards, but I needed to find something for him to do. Luke had already been in and checked them. I made sure there was water and removed any soiled blankets, replacing them with clean ones.

"Okay, let's go check the ones in the back room. Those are the ones who were here before Christmas and still haven't been adopted."

"I counted twenty-eight puppies – they move so fast I may have counted the same ones twice though. Only two have red ribbons. That's good, right?"

"Yes." I walked into the back room and stopped. "Good morning, Lacie. This is my husband, Brett."

She glared at me and then addressed Brett. "Good morning, Detective." She emphasized the 'detective' part and glared at me again.

"So what can we do to help?"

With a side glance to me, she hissed, "Stay away from me."

Ignoring her tone, my response was task oriented. I wasn't going to take her comments personally. "We'll go check on the dogs on the other side, then."

I turned around and walked away. Brett hesitated before he followed me. I sighed with relief as I took a mental check on who was there. What had been smaller dogs was now a mix of small, medium, and large. I recognized the medium and large dogs from the garage. Progress. Checking the clipboards, I directed Brett to take dogs out and cleaned up everything inside the crates, refilled bowls, and added to the laundry pile.

"Aren't they just beautiful? All my babies here and looking for new homes. Justine would be pleased, Lacie too. Here's some fresh dog biscuits for them. Be careful of Horatio and Ghost over there."

She handed me the biscuits and flitted back out. We worked as a team. When we got to Horatio, a Dane mix with his leg in a cast, he didn't bound out of the crate like the others had done. A notation on the clipboard explained his condition. Ghost, a smaller dog, also had a cast.

"I guess we're done. Luke and Blake are taking care of those two. They have to be carefully lifted up and then taken outside. Horatio's a big boy."

We stopped back in the kitchen area. "Mrs. Chantilly, I think you've got it all under control. We did notice a couple of pups with red ribbons. Is Dr. Barksdale tending to them as well as Horatio and Ghost?"

"Vanna is such a wonderful person. She let Lacie work in her hospital for a while. Great opportunity for a young person, you know. Those pups are doing better but need more hand feeding than others. They'll make it. You'll see, Lacie, too."

I wasn't sure if she meant Lacie would also see it or if she'd also make it. I opted not to ask.

"We're going to take off now. We have those errands to run."

"You do that, dears. I hear Justine's children are in town. That Jacob? The dogs don't like him and neither do I. Never calls his mother either. Good for nothing, if you ask me."

She turned back to her baking and with another "good bye," we left. We had a quick lunch at Al's.

117

After we ordered, I waited to hear Brett's observations.

"How'd Lacie know I was a detective? Could be from Mrs. Chantilly. Did you fill out any paperwork to volunteer?"

"Sure. Basic information, but not what you did for a living."

"I bet it included your address? And both she and Lacie would know what your car looked like."

I nodded, realizing his train of thought. Lacie did have access to my address and would recognize my car.

"What would her motive be?"

"For killing Justine? No idea. For resenting you and your involvement in the case? Jealousy? You're working with the chief, not her. You took over how to handle all the dogs and Mrs. Chantilly counts on you for that."

I picked at my burger before I answered him. "But she barely talked to Mrs. Chantilly in the past several years? And at least twice she's gotten angry with Mrs. Chantilly that I witnessed. And… and, she's certainly not doing anything to help prove she's innocent."

Our conversation was cut short as Blake Buchanan walked in and sauntered over to our table, all smiles.

"Well, well, they give you a day off, Detective?" His tone was tempered with sarcasm. Twice now, Brett had been involved in legal situations with Blake's youngest son, Shane. He was doing time for murder as a result.

"Took some personal time to enjoy Sheridan's company. And help out with the Stoneham place."

"Sheridan has been a great help at Pets and Paws, for sure. What's happening at the Stoneham place today?"

Not liking to be talked about or around, I interjected, "Helen and Jacob are in town. They're going to try to clean it out, part of it anyway. I offered to help and Brett's adding another pair of strong arms for all those boxes."

"That's very neighborly of you. Have they figured out what they'll do with the property, yet?"

"No, they haven't found the will yet. Your family has real estate. Ever heard of JJ Properties?"

His face turned red and he opened his mouth and shut it. We waited and after a few seconds, he finally answered.

"They're an arm to a big conglomerate. They buy up properties to create a mega complex with high rises, townhouses, strip malls, and such. They put small family-owned businesses out of business and make a fortune doing so. They wanted to buy up all that land where you folks live when I was mayor, you know. Different realtor company and different name, but same people behind the corporation. Clover Hill has too many zoning requirements and I refused to budge for exceptions on any of them. They popping up again?"

I shrugged. "Not sure. I heard the name mentioned and just wondered who they were."

I could almost see in his eyes as he looked from me to Brett and back how he was processing the conversation. I was not surprised by his next comment.

"Those zoning regulations don't apply to the Stoneham place. Not with all the confusion on the property lines. I have some free time this afternoon. And I'm their nearest neighbor, after all. I'll stop by and see what I can do to help them out.

CHAPTER 21

We arrived at the house and Brett stood outside the car and looked around. He nodded to the officer and approached him.

"Good thing the sun's shining. It's pretty cold out here."

"Yes, sir, it is."

"We were supposed to meet Chief Peabody here. Any idea when he'll be here?"

"He's on his way, sir."

"Anyone else been here yet?"

The man grimaced. "Yes, sir. Mr. Stoneham showed up early. Said he wanted to look for something. I told him he couldn't go in without the chief. He wasn't happy. The chief came and straightened him right out. After Mr. Stoneham left, the chief left to get some breakfast. He should be back shortly."

Brett nodded. "Okay if Sheridan and I take a walk around the house?"

"That should be fine. Inside is a crime scene. Not outside. Mr. Buchanan brought an all-wheel vehicle out and rode the perimeter of the property earlier this week. Found some more dogs in a shed. I'm glad he found them. Not sure they'd have made it otherwise."

"We won't be going that far. Just to get perspective from the outside of the house."

The officer nodded and I joined Brett as he strode to the side of the house.

"Be careful. The ground isn't as flat as it looks. It's kind of uneven."

"I guess they didn't clear the land and put down grass back when they established the 'yard' and the driveway. Any idea how far into the woods their property goes?"

"No. If Blake rode the perimeter, he must have gotten a copy of the plot map and guessed. There's no sign a surveyor has actually come out and marked the property line."

"Why would there be a shack back there?"

Brett shrugged. "They may have left the woods with hopes of being able to hunt in their own backyard. Used the shack when Herman and Jacob went hunting. If they took dogs with them to hunt, the dogs might have known how to get there? If you think of it, mention the shack at some point. Maybe Jacob will volunteer the information."

"Ha! I doubt that. It might prompt the chief to ask about it or Helen might say something about it. Jacob mentioned a rifle. Would that be for hunting and possibly in that shack?"

Brett stopped and shook his head. "Hopefully not. Blake might know since he collected the dogs."

"Obviously, Dan only kept this part cleared and mowed. How much land is this?"

"From the mailbox to the woods past the pile of dirt and out to both sides? Easily a half-acre, maybe more. And that doesn't include any of the woods."

I looked at the woods and thought I saw movement in the trees. Probably a trick of the sun and shadows, but I hoped Blake's dogs had checked the woods. Brett turned around and stared at the rear of the house. We could see the back door and the windows. From this side, it looked like they were boarded half-way up – I was pretty sure the brown wasn't boards, but boxes.

Brett turned back around, his hand out to the side. We both waited and then heard the engine of what sounded like a truck. Brett shook his head.

"I thought I saw movement. Did you see something, too?"

"Maybe. It's gone now, whatever it was. Come on. Let's see who just arrived."

As we circled around the house, we saw a truck with a dumpster in tow. Brett joined the driver and the officer. After much discussion, the driver in a hurry, the dumpster was deposited a couple of yards from the porch. With a good arm, maybe they could throw boxes into the dumpster from the porch. As the driver left, three cars came in – the chief, Helen, and Jacob had arrived.

The chief got out of his car and nodded in our direction. If he was surprised to see Brett, he didn't let it show. Helen next and then Jacob.

"What are they doing here? If I couldn't go in…"

"Hi, Chief. We've been waiting for you to arrive." Brett turned to Helen and Jacob. "I'm Sheridan's husband, Brett. It sounded like you might need some muscle to move boxes, so I came along to help."

Helen smiled and glanced at me. I smiled back. Jacob bristled. He trembled head to toe. "Fine. You'll do as I say. Let's go."

He stormed off and didn't wait for the chief to give him the go ahead before walking in. The chief and Brett followed him.

"Helen, how about you and I check the boxes out here and clean off the porch?" I for one was looking to avoid going inside. It had warmed up a little and the stench was not so putrid on the porch.

She nodded and we easily established that most of the loose stuff was ads and junk mail. We quickly sorted out what might be bills or bank statements and placed them to one side, held down with a rock. Loose pieces of paper, I couldn't throw them and expect them to all land in the dumpster. I called to the officer.

"Excuse me. Could you give us a hand? If we give you stuff, can you put it in the dumpster for us?"

He nodded and we handed off what we could. The boxes were more of the same. It looked like she'd used boxes from the deliveries until she ran out of boxes and then just stacked everything on top.

"Helen, now that you have everything out of that box? How about we use it to put the 'save for later' stuff in?"

She nodded and put the papers we'd loaded down with a loose rock into the now empty box. The next box we each emptied, we left empty. That way we could sort from one box to the other and throw the whole box out. We worked pretty steadily and after an hour or so, more of the porch was clear. Brett came out and whistled.

"You ladies have a system and you've made a dent. Sheridan can I take you away from this – for the sake of all our sanity?"

I looked at him not sure what he was talking about. "Huh?"

"Can you make a quick run to the nearest convenience store and pick up six coffees – get them all black with cream and sugar on the side to make it easy. Unless Helen wants something else?"

"No, coffee would be wonderful."

"Got it, and I'll grab some waters, too." No one ever needs to suggest a coffee run to me more than once.

CHAPTER 22

He handed me the keys and I left. Within twenty minutes I was back and the first coffee went to the officer who'd been helping us. Then Helen took one and what she needed. Mine was already fixed and I set it on a box.

"Our table. Now to venture inside."

Helen nodded and I walked in the doorway. What had been a clean path was now a mess. No other way to describe it. I could see the top of Brett's head midway into the stacks.

"Coffee service here."

"Coming." Brett answered and I watched his head as he side-stepped to where the path had been and came toward me.

"Not as efficient as your method. We're just rearranging boxes to check out closets. So far, the one near the front door didn't have the safe he thinks he remembers. Thanks for the coffee."

I nodded and tilted my head as someone else approached.

"Here you go. I'll keep working with Helen." I'm not sure why, but I reached up and kissed him before I went back outside. Helen was working on a box close to the door, and I picked up a stack of loose mail from the floor and handed it to her as I came out.

"Loose stuff all over the floor in there. Might as well add it to the box you're on. I'll keep working on my end."

With our system, we worked steadily and even moved boxes so we could sit while we sorted. After about three hours we had the porch cleared other than our "seats" and the one box, now almost full, of mail that might need to be opened and shredded.

"Relax for a few minutes. There's bottled water in that bag if you're thirsty. Not as good as coffee, but ..."

Helen exhaled and grabbed a water. I returned to the fray. I looked around and other than some stacks higher than others and loose mail and newspaper on the floor, I couldn't see anyone.

"Anyone want water?"

"Upstairs. I'll come down – don't even try to come up." I could hear the disdain in Brett's voice. I picked up the loose stuff off the floor in front of me for a couple of feet and brought it out to Helen. I went back inside, bag in one hand, and used my feet to move as much loose stuff as possible into a pile. Brett suddenly appeared in front of me. Seeing what I was doing, he started pushing the stuff in my direction. We met up and I handed him the bag of water.

"Heads up. We have to get home – at least one of us – in the next hour."

He nodded and whispered, "He's one of a kind and not the good kind."

He turned and walked away. I picked up the papers and brought them out to Helen.

"Brett and I can only stay..."

A car pulled in and I recognized it immediately. Blake Buchanan had arrived. The officer stopped him at the car. I yelled in the door, "Blake Buchanan is here."

Then I sat with Helen, whose mouth dropped, and waited. Blake joined us on the porch, the officer trotting behind him.

"I'm not going in, just paying my respects to these lovely ladies. Hello, Sheridan. And you must be Helen. I dare say the last time I saw you, you were a toddler. I'm Blake Buchanan and I'm sorry for your loss."

Helen hesitated when faced with his southern charm and smile. "Thank you, Mr. Buchanan. And thank you for your assistance in finding ..."

Her voice broke and before she could regain her composure, Jacob bellowed, "Get off my property, you slime ball. Who do you think you are? You could care less about us or our parents."

By then Jacob was on the porch. Obviously, he wasn't used to heavy exertion and had been sweating. A new odor to add to the smells. His face was red, his breathing heavy, and his fists clenched.

Brett moved around Jacob and nodded to Blake. The chief came out last. He looked to Jacob. "You may not be aware of it, however Mr. Buchanan has been extremely helpful. If not for his dogs, we wouldn't have found your parents at all."

Jacob looked at Blake and sneered. "So what brings you out here this time?"

"I wanted to stop and pay my respects, offer my condolences, and see if I could help in any way." He shrugged like his reasons were obvious.

Jacob took a step forward and both Brett and the chief positioned themselves to intervene if necessary.

"We don't need your respect or condolences or any help from a Buchanan. Your kind play dirty and you just want our land. You probably killed my father and mother to get it. Chief, why haven't you arrested him? He's guilty as sin."

The chief let him rant and put up his hand. "Blake, I don't think you're welcome here right now. I certainly appreciate all the help you've provided. Please be on your way."

Blake opened his mouth to speak, thought better of it, and left.

"Mr. Stoneham. There is no evidence that Blake or any member of his family had anything to do with your parents' deaths. In fact, I would remind you that your father's death was determined to be of natural causes. Without facts or evidence, you'd best be careful of making accusations."

Jacob raised his hand slightly and the chief put his hand up to signal him to stop.

"We've been at this for hours. We're all tired and we need a break. I don't see this all going anywhere." He looked around the porch and smiled. "These ladies need to share their system – fine job out here."

"Chief? The box over there is mail I'd like to look at – get account numbers from, you know. Can I take that box with me?"

"Yes, ma'am. You can."

"No, she can't. Not until I make sure the will or legal papers aren't in there." Jacob grabbed for the box and the contents went flying.

"See what you made me do!" He lunged for Helen and tripped as Brett's well-placed leg got in his way.

I put the papers back into the box and handed the box to the chief. He thumbed through the envelopes. "Electric company. Chewy's dog supplies. Meals-To-Go. Chevron bill. And more of the same. Nothing from an attorney. And Helen, you need to contact Chewy's and Meals-To-Go and cancel the orders, as soon as possible."

She nodded and turned to leave.

"Can we plan on meeting here again at nine tomorrow morning?"

Brett and I exchanged nods before he answered in the affirmative. Jacob and Helen nodded. Tired and cold, we followed Helen down the driveway. Before she left us, she handed me a piece of paper with her phone number and asked me to call her later. It was after dinner, with Maddie in her room, when I called Helen back with my number blocked and the phone on speaker.

"Hi, Helen. Sheridan Hendley here. You asked me to call?"

"Yes. I wanted to thank you for your support and help these past few days, among other things. I didn't want to talk at the house where Jacob might have heard me. I met with the manager at the bank this morning and turned in a copy of the letter from the coroner, attesting to my father's death. There's some hold up on the actual death certificate, but that was sufficient."

"And, what were you able to find out?"

"His checks have been autodeposited and I have a listing of all the autopays from the account. The bank manager cancelled the debit card effective immediately when I told him we didn't have a clue where it was. I asked him to freeze the account until it was all straightened out with who inherited. He … You were right. He said the banking aspect was not part of the estate. I was the only other person on the account."

"That's one less thing to worry about, though you need to deal with all the autopay accounts."

"I managed to reach some of them before we came to the house today. The coroner also helped me with setting up funeral arrangements. Jacob plans to go home to Atlanta on Wednesday, so I'm scheduling the services and memorial for Tuesday. That was the soonest I could arrange for burial in the family plots in Oak Grove."

"Good. You are making decisions and you'll be able to get some closure."

"I can deal with accounting and banking and such. There are rules and procedures. Jacob is the problem. That and the open investigation. I know you're helping the chief. Are there any other questions you need to ask?"

I hesitated and looked to Brett. Then I remembered the one question we had. "One thing we wondered about. There's apparently a shack in the woods out back. Do you remember it or know what it was used for?"

She chuckled. "Different things at different times. When I was little I asked for a treehouse or a life size doll house or something. The shack was my place to play when my parents wanted me or both of us out of the way. I remember it most from that time. It was closed in and had a bathroom and small fridge. Most of my dolls and stuffed animals lived there. My father didn't like clutter."

"That's interesting. That your dolls and animals had their own house, I mean."

"As I got older, and Jacob got bigger, his trucks and stuff took over and it wasn't as much fun. I didn't like being there with him alone. He was always mean to me."

"What happened after that?"

"After a while, I'd refuse to go there. I'd play outside instead. Sometimes, my mother would tell us dad went away on a business trip, but I figured out sometimes he stayed in the shack. In high school, I caught them both in the shack. Embarrassing then," she laughed, "kind of funny now."

On our end, we both smiled. "Can you think of any other hideaways your dad or mom had? Any place he might have stashed his will?"

"Afraid not. Other than the house, the shack, and the bank, occasionally to church, I don't think he ever went anywhere. My mom only left the house to get groceries and run errands related to the house. Growing up, I watched how she catered to my dad and swore I wouldn't end up in that kind of relationship."

"Let us know if you think of anything else and we'll see you in the morning."

CHAPTER 23

Melina came by promptly at half past eight. Amazingly, Maddie was dressed and ready to go. Of course, she and Nedra would be playing with the pups all morning and then playing at Melina's house until we finished up at the Stoneham place. Or ran out of energy or patience or both. We'd discussed what song she'd sing for the tryouts and I suspected the dogs and anyone else around would be her captive audience.

Brett and I stopped at Dunkin' and got a large thermos of coffee as well as individual coffees for us and a dozen donuts. I gobbled up a cinnamon roll before we even got to the Stoneham place. This time we arrived after the chief and Helen. No sign of Jacob. I wasn't sorry.

It wasn't too cold and, to create space inside, Brett and the chief moved boxes out to the porch, stacked three high. Then they went to work using our system of working from a box to the floor and then using the empty box to sort out the next box. It was a different officer, but he was so thankful for the coffee and donuts, he was happy to be our conduit to the dumpster.

We worked steadily with minimal conversation. When Jacob still wasn't there an hour later, I asked, "Did you talk to Jacob at all last night or this morning?"

She huffed. "He called me around midnight, yelling in a drunken rage. I hung up on him. He's probably hung over."

We worked some more and she stood up, paper falling to the porch floor.

"What did you find?"

"I'm not sure. The return address looks like an attorney to me." She handed it to me.

"Greenspan, Morrison, Grant, and Lane. Definitely could be an attorney. Better let the chief know."

She took the letter and went inside. I decided it was time for a stretch and walked as far as the doorway. Brett had been walking past us with box after box and it was now apparent just how many boxes. There was now a lane at least five boxes wide and four deep. I could see there was a table under the boxes on my right. Most importantly, the front windows were no longer obstructed and light filtered in.

Brett joined me while the chief and Helen had a private conversation. I whispered, "Furniture" and tapped the table. He smiled. The chief and Helen joined us.

"I've put a call in to the number for this firm and asked them to return my call regarding Herman and Justine. Hopefully, their answering service will get them the message and realize this is not a 'wait until we have time' phone call. In the meantime, I'll hold onto this."

Helen and I resumed our work out on the porch after coffee refills. When we'd cleaned off the porch, we joined the men inside. We all stopped when the chief's phone rang.

"Uh huh. Yes. I understand. Thank you for the notification." He hung up and shook his head.

"That was someone from the next police district – Oak Grove. Jacob was stopped for driving under the influence and spent the night as their guest. When he took off his shirt – he got sick on himself – they noticed scratches and a puncture wound on his arm. They're holding him until the local doctor can check it out. He's already claiming police brutality and threatening to sue, so he'll be completely checked out before he's released."

He rolled his eyes and then smiled. I didn't ask what "completely checked out" meant.

"I knew he was drunk when he called. I'm glad they picked him up. But why was he in Oak Grove? I wonder if he visited the cemetery and the family plots."

I shrugged. "Guess we keep working. Though, um… Can we move some of the boxes to get to the bathroom?"

Brett laughed. "Upstairs. We had to get access yesterday. It works and it's not too bad. There's even toilet paper."

I went upstairs and gasped. As downstairs, what had been a relatively neat stacking of boxes, was now random. I managed to step over and around boxes to get to the bathroom. While there, I checked the vanity drawers – only the usual bathroom stuff. I knew it was a longshot, likely a function of too much television and murder mysteries, yet I lifted the lid of the commode to check for anything hidden there. Nothing. Disappointed, I made my way back downstairs.

By noon, we all found boxes to sit on and relaxed. We'd uncovered the front of a sofa Helen remembered and the coffee table. She smiled but with a sadness in her eyes as she looked around what was once again beginning to look like what she remembered of her childhood home.

"Pizza anyone? Fresh coffee?" The chief looked at each of us as we nodded. Then he called in the order. Three large pizzas, six coffees, and lots of napkins.

"We have bottled water in the car, too."

"Have you found anything interesting yet?" Helen asked the men.

The chief snorted. "We discovered the downstairs bathroom. Still works though obviously wasn't being used." He hesitated. "Jacob mentioned a small gun safe. Do you have any recollection of where that might have been?"

"Not really, but I'm thinking it was in their room. The room…" She turned a little green again.

"Put your head between your knees. It'll pass in a few minutes. Do you know how a water brigade works?"

We nodded and the chief continued. "Okay we've cleaned up some space here and the stairs are clear. I think we need to form a brigade and pass boxes down from the master bedroom to the hall upstairs and get them down here and out on the porch. Helen, you can stay down here and keep sorting. If Jacob shows up, holler and I'll get my officer back outside fast. While we wait on the pizza, Brett and I will start moving the boxes from in front of the master bedroom to the stairs. Sound like a plan?"

All in agreement, the two of them disappeared upstairs. I followed behind and grabbed up all the loose stuff in the hall. Brett brought the first box downstairs for Helen to work on and the chief followed with another. As we worked, we could hear them moving around upstairs, moving boxes to the stairs. When the pizza arrived, we yelled and they came down, each carrying a box.

Tired and hungry, there wasn't much conversation. The chief called the officer outside to come in and eat with us. The pizza was hot, the coffee was fresh, and we were sated in no time. Unfortunately, Brett and the officer had all the boxes they'd already moved to the stairs downstairs quicker than we could dispose of them. Then the brigade began. The chief would take a box to Brett to the officer to me to Helen. About ten boxes later, I saw movement outside and yelled "Incoming."

All three men were downstairs in a heartbeat, each with a box. The chief and officer went outside. Brett looked to me his brows raised.

"I didn't see a car. I saw a person dart from our car to behind Helen's. I don't know if it was Jacob or not. I thought I saw someone in the woods yesterday too. This time I can tell you they had a blue jacket on."

He nodded and stood in the doorway. Helen and I watched the scene outside through the dirty windows. We watched the two men in the yard signal each other and heard the chief when he said, "You can't sneak away. Whoever you are, come out and explain yourself right now."

We all walked out onto the porch. Nothing happened for a few seconds and then the chief shook his head. "Lacie, what are you doing here?"

"I came … I came to see what was going on. You seem to think I killed Justine and I can't go to work. Dora doesn't need me and she makes me crazy anyway."

"Wait. Aren't you the housekeeper who was helping my mother out?"

Lacie nodded. "Until Herman retired. Then he said she didn't need help."

"That's not quite consistent with the payment records we found, Lacie."

She shrugged. "Every once in a while, Justine'd call when Herman wasn't around and I'd come out. But not weekly like before."

The chief stared at her, as if waiting for something else. She didn't say another word. Just turned to walk off.

"Lacie. My office. Let me know when it's convenient. I expect you to arrange for it before Monday morning."

She turned around and nodded. Then she disappeared from my view.

"Did you see where she went?"

Brett shook his head. "The driveway curves just enough that she vanished. She must have parked on the road."

"Okay, folks. In another hour, we should be able to get into the bedroom." He turned to the officer. "John, you need to stay out here. Just keep helping the ladies get the boxes into the dumpster."

We followed the chief into the house. The chief and Brett brought boxes and we sorted and sorted. The officer stayed outside but continued to take boxes from us to the dumpster. I knew they'd made it into the room when Brett took one parcel of stuff out the door. It looked like sheets all folded up.

Chief Peabody followed him and grunted. "Not as young as I used to be. Jacob still hasn't made it here and I think it's time to call it a day. I think it'll only take a couple of hours to get to the master bath and closet. Anyone game for tomorrow?"

I looked to Brett and he nodded. "We can be here. That's definitely the most likely place to find a will or legal documents."

He paused and turned to Helen. "I'm afraid after that, you'll be on your own. I'd suggest hiring some high school boys, starting with Dan who did the yard work around here. Just to cart the boxes downstairs."

The chief added, "I'll arrange to have the dumpster replaced with a fresh one on Monday. That one will be full by tomorrow."

"Okay. I appreciate your help. I doubt Jacob will do much. And Chief Peabody, I already told Brett and Sheridan, I tentatively planned a service for my father on Tuesday. Jacob said he's returning to Atlanta on Wednesday."

The chief's mouth flattened out and he hesitated before he responded. "Please let me know what the arrangements are tomorrow. Will one o'clock work for everyone?" We all nodded. "Then let's get out of here."

He stopped to talk to the officer after closing the door. We headed home, tired and in need of showers.

CHAPTER 24

Sunday morning was intentionally laid back and a breakfast casserole made food preparation a breeze. Brett immediately went into the garage to work on organization, a seemingly never ending task.

No surprise, Maddie slept as I pulled all the laundry together, changed sheets, and cleaned up the kitchen. Charlie hung out with me. Bella had gone back to bed with Maddie.

Pleased with my progress, I relaxed on the couch and tried to think through the last few days, connecting all the players. I jumped up when I remembered something Mrs. Chantilly said.

"Did I scare you? I didn't mean to." Brett tilted his head, hands up as he joined me.

"No. No, you didn't scare me. I just remembered something Mrs. Chantilly said. How did she know Jacob didn't like dogs?"

He shrugged. "Maybe she was remembering from when he was a child? Or confused Jacob and Herman?"

My excitement deflated, I sat back down. "I guess that's possible. It's always hard to get a time frame when she says something. I may ask about it just to be sure. We may have to stop there again to see how things are going before we go to the Stoneham house."

"And Maddie? We still in agreement she stays home and works on her room, her closet, and her laundry? I'm not thinking we'll be there more than three hours. If we don't find the safe before then, I'll chalk it up to his imagination."

"I think you're right and they'll need to figure out what they want to keep or sell or give away."

"Sher, please don't go over there without the chief or me or someone else. I'm less than impressed with Jacob's attitudes or behavior. He's a potential danger."

"Agreed. Even if he didn't kill her, he isn't one of the good guys, either. Tomorrow I have meetings at Millicent most of the day anyway. I told Helen I'd go to the memorial on Tuesday. Kind of cold, if you ask me, that Jacob's already leaving – and leaving the work for Helen."

"He may have to for his job though. Most employers only allow a limited number of days for a death in the family. We don't know his situation."

I nodded as Maddie joined us. With directions to the casserole, she ate and we reminded her of her chores. She groaned but our united front was too strong. We left her with a to-do list and drove to Pets and Paws. Inside it was busy, Mrs. Chantilly smiling and carrying her famous homemade dog biscuits as she bounced from room to room.

"Well, hello, Sheridan, Brett? Have you reconsidered getting another dog? We have a great variety."

"Afraid not, Mrs. Chantilly. Charlie and Bella are more than enough. We just wanted to stop by and see how things were going."

"Have you cleared Lacie yet? The dogs are doing fine. An adoption day will do the trick. We've already had interest in the puppies. Maybe I should bring one of Justine's dogs to the memorial." She shook her head. "No, Jacob would be upset."

Brett poked me. "Jacob? As in Herman and Justine's son?"

"Oh, yes. Rosco doesn't like him at all. Growled. Bared his teeth. That quiet, gentle dog. But then Jacob was yelling and his language? I think Rosco was offended. Luke managed to get him calmed down – Rosco that is. Then that nice lady came and Rosco was so happy. Sometimes you have to let them go. Blake says I need to let Lacie go."

I opened my mouth and closed it, trying to formulate the right question. "Was Jacob here this past week? I didn't see him."

"Of course, what do you think I've been telling you? He is not like a fine wine. Did not improve with age. I'm not a drinker – I don't really know how true it is about wine. Do you lovebirds drink wine?"

"Occasionally. I wonder why he came by?"

"Yelling, screaming. Luke was here and walking Rosco. It was … I don't know. It's time to make biscuits. Luke's in charge of the volunteer schedule. He's doing just a wonderful job." She smiled and walked away, head high. Luke had walked up and nodded.

Brett and I turned to Luke. He dragged his hand across his face.

"You want to know about Jacob and Rosco?" He spoke very quietly, his eyes on Mrs. Chantilly's disappearing back.

We nodded and he continued. "I came around the side of the house with Rosco – he was happy, full of energy and we both needed the exercise."

He shrugged, almost apologetic. "This man was waving his arms and screaming at Mrs. C, saying it was all her fault. He wasn't making much sense – he argued that Justine was copying her. Rosco started growling before I could even see who it was."

He shook his head. "They came into view and Jacob took a step closer. I could barely hold onto Rosco. He went ballistic. Jacob jumped back, grabbed his arm, and dove for his car. Couldn't get out of here fast enough. As soon as he was in the car and out of sight, Rosco stopped trying to get to him but he growled until the car left."

Brett and I exchanged glances. "Do you remember what day that was?"

He shrugged. "Those days after the first batch of dogs, more dogs, and then they found Justine, and then still more dogs? Sorry, I lost track of what day it was. Somewhere in the middle of the chaos. Somehow when nobody else was here. Not you, not Blake, not Lacie." He hung his head.

"Luke, you were sleep walking part of that time. If not for you…"

"Young man, you did more than you had to. Don't beat yourself up over not remembering who did what when."

He hung his head. "Thanks. Only I still can't ...I think I blacked out or something. I was busy logging in dogs that first day and keeping track. You were here Dr. H., and Ms. Melina, tagging the dogs. You all left and I did a quick check in the garage and then took care of our dogs, the mamas and pups, and the smaller ones. By then I figured I needed to do one more check of the garage."

He looked away and then shrugged. "There were like six dogs, not even in crates. All huddled in the corner, shaking. I don't remember bringing them down there – they hadn't been bathed or fed. They weren't on my log, but there they were. One of them had a broken leg. That's why I called him Ghost."

I knew my eyes widened and Brett showed the same surprise I felt. Covering for my surprise, I tried to make him feel better, even if it didn't make any more sense to me than to him.

"You called it chaos before and that's the best description."

Brett cleared his throat. "Luke, was the garage door locked?"

"The main garage door was down, except for the last couple inches. The back door was unlocked and the vents were open. The garage is heated and we wanted to be sure there was air circulation and easy access if there was a problem. Mrs. C. didn't remember the last time the heater had been used. The plan was for me to check on them and the heater before I left, grab a couple of hours sleep, and then come back early."

He turned to me. "You know how that turned out."

"You never left or slept. You took care of those other dogs, didn't you? Again, you did more than anyone for these dogs and Mrs. C. How long do you think you were tied up in the house before you went back to check?"

"Two hours. Maybe a little more."

"Had Lacie stopped in before then?"

He grimaced. "She stopped by briefly to check in with Mrs. C. They went down to the garage together. Then she left, promising to return the next day. She insulted me and called me one of Mrs. C.'s rescues. Like she should talk. Mean-spirited and cold."

Brett nodded and then glanced at his watch. "Alarm just went off – we need to book."

I gave Luke a half hug and Brett patted his shoulder as we left. He was no longer the cocky, entitled, and obnoxious teen of last summer.

CHAPTER 25

By the time we reached the Stoneham house, it was a little past one o'clock. Three other cars beat us there. We didn't spot the police officer on guard and went inside. Voices drifted down from upstairs, mostly Jacob's, loud and hostile.

"… what if the will was in that envelope? Police are crooked. You stupid…"

"Mind your language, Mr. Stoneham. The envelope was turned over to appropriate authorities along with your contact information. Obviously, the attorney was contacted and in turn got in touch with both of you."

We made it up the stairs as Chief Peabody finished. His face was flushed and Helen was cowering. Preston, the officer from the first day, stood on alert, his hand hovering near his gun. He nodded as we approached.

"Any luck finding that safe yet?" Brett asked, immediately taking the attention off of Jacob and the chief.

The chief's stance relaxed. "Nope. We were about to explain to Jacob about the brigade to get all these boxes out of here and downstairs. Sheridan, can you and Helen handle downstairs and Preston here will help with the dumpster."

I smiled my best fake smile and reached for Helen's arm. She didn't need any encouragement. She slid behind Preston, never taking her eyes off her brother. We headed downstairs, Preston behind us. Brett had the last leg of the brigade to get boxes to us and grimaced as he brought down the first box.

As Helen and I worked, I tried to make conversation. Small talk isn't my strength though.

"How are you holding up?"

"Okay. I talked to my son and daughter last night. They weren't close to their grandparents but it was good to talk to them and talk out some of my confusion. Both encouraged me to stand up to Jacob."

"At the very least, Helen, you need to protect yourself and your interests. Have you given any thought to getting an attorney?"

She smiled. "I mentioned that to my son and he found one for me. I'll be talking to her tomorrow morning." She shook her head.

"So what's the problem?"

"Just when I was feeling a little more in control, Jacob called. He started yelling how he needed money. He went on and on about how Justine got in the way of his getting the house and property. Our parents are dead and that's all he can talk about. I don't want to deal with him. He's so angry. He scares me."

I nodded. There wasn't much I could say. As if it would make a difference, Helen and I attacked the boxes with renewed vigor until Preston came in and looked upstairs. I raised my eyebrows and he signaled out the window. A man in a suit was walking toward the patio, briefcase in hand. I immediately pegged him as an attorney. I was wrong. Preston moved to the stairwell and took the next box from Brett.

"Can you let Mr. Stoneham know someone from JJ Properties is here for him?"

Brett glanced past us and out the window, nodded, and disappeared. In a few minutes, the chief and Jacob came back down. Not surprisingly, only the chief carried a box down. Jacob marched past Helen and me without a word and the chief clenched his jaw.

The chief turned to Helen. "Helen, this may concern you. I think you need to step outside, too."

She looked to me and I went with her.

"... Benjamin Jordan, Mr. Stoneham. Call me Ben. We were sorry to hear of your loss yet happy to be of service in helping you resolve... er, address... the property so you can move on with your life. Shall we?" He waved his arm toward the house and I stifled a laugh.

Jacob faltered. "I'm ... I'm afraid there are some complications here. You might have noticed the police officer. I wasn't aware of these things when I called."

That was the chief's cue. "I'm Chief Peabody, Mr. Jordan. A woman was murdered here and it is still a crime scene. The other thing Mr. Stoneham may not have mentioned is the absence of legally binding documents giving him full rights to dispose of property without the agreement of his sister, Helen." He extended his arm in Helen's direction.

Jacob's face got red and Mr. Jordan took a step backward. "In that case, I guess any discussion at this time is premature. Please contact our office when ownership is resolved." His nose twitched and he turned, disappearing down the driveway.

"Any headway upstairs?" I asked, hoping to diffuse Jacob's rising anger.

"Only another five or six boxes and we should be able to get into the closet." The chief shrugged. "I just hope there aren't more boxes in the closet, blocking this supposed safe."

Jacob took a step forward – matched quickly by Brett and Preston. "It's there. I remember it. He kept his guns and ammo and papers in it."

"Let's go find it then."

I watched as they marched in. It wasn't too much longer and Brett brought down yet another box.

"We found the safe. A small gun safe in the back of the closet. Either Jacob doesn't know the combination or he won't tell anyone. Peabody keeps trying birthdays, wedding dates. Helen, do you have any idea what numeric combination your dad might have used?"

"No. Afraid not. Did they try something as simple as 1-2-3-4?"

Brett's mouth twitched as he tried not to laugh. "Your father was smart enough to change it. On the plus side, we found a key to the house in the bathroom. The door can be locked now and Chief Peabody will hold the key."

I nodded and Helen added, "That's good. I never had a key. I'm not sure about Jacob. He certainly hasn't volunteered that he has a key."

We heard grumbling and all three of us watched as the chief came down the stairs, Jacob ranting at him.

"This is my house. I should have the key. I don't care what you say."

"Mr. Stoneham, until the courts tell me otherwise, I am keeping the key. We will lock the door as we walk out. Personally, I want to go home and catch the football game."

Brett nodded. "We need to get home as well and a football game sounds good."

I groaned for effect, though I would be watching with him. Most importantly, it was time to leave and see what was happening with Maddie.

At home, we found Maddie asleep on the couch, Bella in her arms and Charlie at her feet. Charlie immediately headed to the back door and I managed to get Bella free without waking Maddie. I put on coffee and started to get dinner ready. Brett joined me within minutes, smiling.

"I'm impressed. It looks like she did everything on the list. The laundry's done, her room's clean, and her bed's made. It looks like she even dusted and vacuumed."

"So it would pass the white glove test, huh? No wonder she's sleeping. Early to bed for me tonight – early morning for boring meetings before the semester starts."

CHAPTER 26

Brett took time off to attend the memorial with me on Tuesday. We had both become protective of Helen given her bully of a brother. We drove into Oak Grove and it had the quaint appeal of older small towns. As we neared the town center, the houses were closer to the road and then were replaced with the Grove Inn, local stores, and then Joe's Bar. We drove past the center of town and turned.

The Crestview Eternal Resting Place was a family cemetery, with areas blocked off for future family members with pre-paid plots. Herman's memorial service wasn't publicized but some of the same people who pretended Herman and Justine didn't exist in life showed up. That included Mrs. Chantilly, Blake and his wife, Mr. Jordan from JJ Properties, and others I didn't recognize. Chief Peabody was there and joined us as we approached the gathering.

He shook his head. "I stopped by the house this morning and someone broke into the house. They..." He made air quotes around "They" and continued,

"Opened the safe. There were papers on the floor, including a family tree, an old Bible, and a map with property lines. No telling what else was or wasn't in the safe."

He grunted and shifted his gaze in the direction of Helen and Jacob. "Not very smart or careful – we managed to get some prints."

He didn't have time to say anything else as a hush fell over the small group. All eyes turned to Pastor Pete. Of all the people present, he was probably the one who had the strongest connection with Herman and Justine.

"It is with sadness but also honor that I speak on this occasion. I've known Herman and Justine for many years – since I first came to Clover Hill. I watched them raise their children, now adults, and grow into their golden years." He chuckled.

"They came to church and participated in activities with the congregation, especially anytime there were hot dogs. Herman loved his hot dogs loaded with mustard. He lived a long and fulfilled life. Let us pray."

As Pastor Pete read scripture, I glanced around. Even though it was winter, the grave sites were well tended. There were obviously some gardens scattered throughout – likely they added color in the spring and summer. Trees created a fence of sorts around the area of the funeral. That's when I spotted Lacie on the fringes, at first almost hidden in the trees and then walking toward us. I elbowed Brett and whispered, "Check out the tree line to my right."

He nodded as Pastor Pete ended with a brief prayer and offered condolences to family members. Neither Jacob nor Helen said anything and people began milling around, speaking quietly among themselves and with Helen. Brett and I slowly made our way to Jacob and Helen to offer our condolences formally. Mrs. Chantilly gravitated to Lacie and hugged her. The quiet peacefulness of the service held until Jacob shattered it.

"You! This is your fault." He bolted in the direction of Lacie and Mrs. Chantilly. Then he grabbed Lacie. "How dare you show up here? I could kill you."

He shook Lacie whose mouth dropped and eyes widened. Brett and the chief both interceded and pulled Jacob away, but not before Jacob nailed Brett in the jaw. Lacie stumbled, bumping into Mrs. Chantilly, who teetered backwards. A man I didn't recognize stopped her from falling. Helen stepped away from Jacob and slipped behind me. Brett signaled me to stay put as he rubbed his jaw.

"You don't understand. That woman. She's the housekeeper. She was supposed to help Justine. This is all her fault. Bad egg. Probably got as much money as she could from her and then killed her."

Jacob managed to move away from the chief and let loose a string of profanity. Pastor Pete moved forward, his face pale. He spoke calmly though and tried to disperse the crowd.

"We all appreciate Jacob's distress. Everyone handles grief differently. Perhaps everyone should move along. Thank you all for coming." His arms spread, he moved forward and tried to herd them away.

The man who had helped Mrs. Chantilly stepped around her, his head tilted as he studied Jacob. He squinted and grimaced.

"Wait a minute. I remember you. Mean temper and mean right hook when I caught you cheating at poker at Joe's a week ago." He rubbed his jaw. "Manny said it was the second time you caused trouble. You disappeared mighty quick. Can't hold your liquor, your mouth, or your temper. One big loser."

Jacob paled and mumbled something I didn't understand.

An older woman stepped forward scowling. "Not just a problem at Joe's. I'm surprised he showed his face here. He's nothing but a bully and drunk and he doesn't pay his bills either. Jerome had to deal with him – I sure wasn't going to. He owes us for his room at the Grove Inn, though he hasn't shown up since last Thursday. Drunk most nights before that."

The woman spoke clearly and directed her comments at the chief. The chief shifted his attention from Jacob to her. In that split second, the next thing we knew, Jacob grabbed Lacie again and pulled a gun.

"Now Jacob, what are you doing? I'm sure you can resolve the issue with the inn. We all know you're under distress right now. Don't make things worse. Somebody could get hurt. Just put the gun down and let Lacie go. What do you say?" The chief kept his voice even and didn't take a step. Nobody else moved either.

Jacob swore and shifted his stance. "Don't anyone move or I'll shoot her. I will."

Helen stepped forward, tears running down her cheeks. "Jacob, think about what you're doing. Chief Peabody is right. Don't make things any worse. So far you haven't done anything bad. We'll work this all out."

He shifted slightly again and I gasped, afraid he was going to turn the gun on Helen. Then Lacie stepped sideways, rolled, and Jacob was on the ground. She kicked the gun away from him and moved away. With no hesitation, the chief had him flipped over and handcuffed. Brett helped to get him standing up and secured the gun.

The chief turned to the woman from the inn. "Ma'am, are you sure this is the man who was staying at your inn until the last few days?"

"I sure am. He initially came in the week before and said he'd be leaving the next Monday. He was staying three days, he said. Saturday to Monday. But he kept extending his checkout date. Since Thursday, he's only been in and out. I don't know where he's been staying. Personally I'm glad he was somewhere else. He was rude and his room reeked."

The chief nodded. "I'll need your contact information so I can get an official statement." He turned toward the man who had spoken up. "Yours, too." Both immediately complied.

Jacob squirmed. And I did the math. He'd been at the Sleep Softly Inn since Thursday. And if he'd arrived the Saturday before that, he'd been in Oak Grove before Justine was killed.

Chief Peabody spoke to the woman again. "I'll need a copy of your records to get the dates right."

"No problem." She must have picked up on the importance of when Jacob arrived and she volunteered, "He's had the rental car the whole time too."

"Jacob, you won't be needing that rental right now. You're coming with me to Clover Hill. Lacie, Preston will escort you since you never managed to get in yesterday on your own." He stared at her until she nodded. Preston moved to her side. Brett accompanied Jacob and the chief to the chief's car.

Some of us stood there and didn't move, others drifted off, convinced the excitement was over. One man stopped by Lacie before moving on. "I have to admit, that was great. How'd you know how to do that?"

Lacie actually smiled. "I work as a police dispatcher and part of the training was in self-defense. You know like if they brought in someone and they managed to get to me. First time I actually had to use it – if he hadn't shifted his position, I'm not sure I'd have been able to take the step and roll."

The man grinned. "Guess the jerk didn't count on that."

As he walked away, I heard Helen mutter, "I need to get some of that self-defense training." I smiled.

CHAPTER 27

The adrenalin rush faded and Brett and I made our excuses. Neither of us said a word until we stopped at Seafood Grill & Deli for lunch. Even though it wasn't crowded, Brett requested a booth in the back. As soon as we were seated and our orders taken, I offered my opinion.

"He could have killed Justine. If the lady from the inn was right, he was in Oak Grove before Justine was killed."

"Here or not, doesn't mean he killed her. It still could have been Lacie."

"Now, Detective," I teased. "Don't you have to identify a motive? He had motive – he wants the property so he can sell it to JJ Properties. What would Lacie's motive be?"

He chuckled. "Maybe Justine had something on her? Owed her money? Maybe she was upset about the dogs? No idea. It does sound like he arrived long before Wednesday. That's the problem with cell phones. The area code doesn't tell you where the person is or where they live even. Who'd think to do a trace if you're calling someone to notify them of a death?"

"Sounds like he was right there in Oak Grove when he got the call that Justine had passed away. And I wondered why his sister could get here from Seattle sooner than he could from Atlanta."

"Any chance Jacob and Helen worked together?"

"I'm sticking to my initial impression. She hadn't seen the house – outside or in – before we met her there. I may not know her whole story and how much she needs the money or if she'd want to sell. Her shock at the condition of the house was real."

Brett's phone rang. "Yes?"

"We're at Seafood Grill & Deli, what would you expect?"

"Got it."

He hung up and signaled the waitress. "Peabody's on his way."

As the waitress approached, he added, "A friend is going to join us. He'd like the shrimp hoagie and chips please. Coffee when he gets here."

She nodded and walked away.

"What'd he say?"

"Jacob answered some questions and then lawyered up."

We'd finished eating when the chief arrived. He pulled up a chair and attacked the sandwich after a rushed "Thank you. How's your jaw?"

"Sore, but I'll live."

A few bites and a sip of coffee later, he shook his head.

"No breakfast and that man tried my patience. He'd spin a tale and then contradict himself. Swore the woman from the Grove Inn was confused and had her dates wrong. Insisted he made the reservation because he didn't want to stay at the house and then forgot to cancel it when I reserved rooms for them here in Clover Hill."

"There must be a way to verify it, right?"

He held his hand up. "I asked about Mr. Bixley. That was the man who implied – and since confirmed – that he caught Jacob cheating in a poker game and got clipped in the jaw as a result. Jacob doesn't remember that at all. Given how drunk he was the other night, I'm not surprised."

"Where'd he get the gun?"

"As I expected, the gun was registered to Herman Stoneham. Jacob's prints matched those on the safe, inside and out. Ammunition was in the rental car. He admitted breaking into the house and opening the safe. He cursed a lot but the gist of it was there was no will or anything that specifically said only he should get the property."

"Did he say why he took the gun? Why he brought it to the memorial service?"

The chief grimaced. "He repeated his belief he'd inherit the property. Said if he was going to be rich, he needed protection."

I shook my head. "What about the law firm?" I secretly hoped there was something in place to favor Helen.

"Standard will. Everything to Justine and then to Jacob and Helen evenly, or to their heirs. The only hitch? It was never signed."

I groaned. "Did you ever find out anything about the scratches and puncture wound? Maybe he makes it a habit of irritating people when he's drunk."

"He didn't recall that either. The doctor who examined him said if he had to guess, it was a from a dog or cat. Maybe the Grove Inn has pets."

The chief ate a few more bites of food. Brett took advantage of the lull and asked, "When did he ask for his attorney?"

The chief snorted. "About the time Preston interrupted and handed me a copy of the car rental agreement. He picked up the car at the airport a week ago Saturday morning. He's been right here in Virginia for more than a week. He only acknowledges the last six days."

He shrugged. "We've asked Mrs. Carter, the woman at the Grove Inn to send us the credit card record and his signature on the registration form. She confirms he arrived that Saturday. Unfortunately, it doesn't prove anything, except he was here and lied."

I groaned. "Too bad he won't confess. He called his attorney?"

"No. He called his sister and asked her to find one for him. He started yelling at her and told her he has no money until he sells the house and property. His phone is now in pieces on the floor. She apparently said she couldn't or wouldn't pay for his attorney. We had to make the calls to get him an attorney on the county. In the meantime? He's our guest."

We nodded. Brett tapped his watch and stood. "Keep us posted. We have a few errands to run before Maddie gets home."

In the car on the way home, Brett set his jaw.

"What's up? Does your jaw hurt?"

"It does. And I'm thinking. All this with Helen and Jacob and their dysfunctional family? It makes me worry about Maddie and what will happen down the road with Victoria."

Victoria was his ex-wife and Maddie's mother. She and Roger were some place in Europe. In six months, the only contact with Maddie had been a quick phone call at Christmas.

He leaned enough to squeeze my leg. "Glad to have you on this adventure with me, Sheridan."

CHAPTER 28

We ran a few errands and were home before Maddie. She came home and went straight to her room. What with spending most of Sunday at the Stoneham house, I hadn't talked to my parents. I decided to rectify that. They were both retired and home most of the time.

"Hi, Mom. How are you and Dad doing?"

"Hello Sheridan. We thought you'd forgotten about us. You know we wait for your call on Sundays."

I groaned to myself. "Yes, I know. There were some deaths, and then the dogs I told you about last week? Very long days and with the college not yet in session, I'm afraid I sometimes lose track of what day it is."

"You need to be careful. Memory loss is a sign of aging, you know. Your father can't seem to remember anything, least of all the things I ask him to do. Funny, he has no trouble remembering his meals."

Smiling, I asked, "Are you getting out some? You need to get some exercise."

"Have you looked at a weather map? You may be having a January thaw down there, but we are knee-deep in snow. One day last week it got up to the 40s and we walked through the slush to see a movie. The center was showing one of those old Doris Day and Rock Hudson movies. They served hot cocoa – sugar free, of course."

"That sounds like fun. I do have a question, Mom. We just got back from a memorial service and one of the problems? No one knows where his will is. I realized I don't remember where your wills are."

"Well, there certainly was a question in there somewhere, I think. We don't plan on dying anytime soon, but yes, Sheridan, we have wills and they are with our attorney, along with all the rest of the paperwork so you, Kayla or Kevin can make decisions when we aren't able. I don't like to think about that happening."

"No, Mom, none of us do. I'm still glad you have it all set, and knowing you, the attorney information is on the contact sheet in the drawer, right?" I chuckled. The rest of the world may use technology, but my parents had a handwritten list of important contacts.

"That's right. I had to redo it when you moved to Clover Hill. It's neat and up to date. It's been good talking to you dear, but your dad sat down at the table and wants his dinner. We'll talk next week – on Sunday, right?"

"That's right."

I disconnected and shook my head. Brett gave me a hug.

"Awkward, huh? I keep avoiding asking my parents or my brothers."

I nodded and checked on our dinner. It was almost dinner time, the roast cooked and table set, when the doorbell sounded. It was Chief Peabody. I hoped it meant good news.

"Come on in. Have you eaten?"

"Thanks. No, but don't worry." He tapped his gut and chuckled. "I'm obviously not starving – Alice feeds me well."

He followed us into the kitchen and I grabbed an extra place setting in case he changed his mind. We all laughed as his stomach disagreed with his words.

Maddie playfully punched his arm. "You'll love Sheridan's roast."

"If you're sure it's not a problem?"

"Not at all. There's plenty."

Food on the table, Maddie asked, "Are all the dogs taken care of now? No more found?"

"Yes, Maddie, all the dogs from the Stoneham place have been found."

"And from what Mrs. C told us Sunday, most have been re-homed in foster care. We'll need to go there on Saturday."

"What about the mamas and pups?"

"We'll see on Saturday, but I think she said even some of the puppies."

Maddie continued to talk about the mamas and pups while we ate. When we finished and we were all silent, she took the cue and disappeared to her room to watch a movie.

The chief leaned back into his chair. "It's been an interesting afternoon. Helen buckled and found him an attorney. Jacob met with the man. The attorney looked about twelve years old. I asked him how much experience he had and he hedged." The chief shook his head. "First murder case, I'd bet."

"So what happened?"

"Well, he convinced Jacob to tell his story, sure he could make a case for voluntary manslaughter."

"Huh?" I didn't understand what that meant.

"According to his statement? He had to drive in this direction for his job and decided to stop in and see his parents. He became distraught when he discovered that his father was dead and buried in the backyard. That and his shock at the condition of the house and all the dogs. He had picked up a loose piece of wood and the next thing he knew he hit his mother with it. Then one of the dogs attacked him and he hit the dog. Other dogs started after him, he freaked out, and drove back to Oak Grove. Said he didn't know she was dead until I called him."

"And that qualifies as manslaughter?"

He rolled his eyes. "The attorney believes that his actions were the result of the heat of passion as a result of reasonable provocation."

"He left her there to die."

The chief shrugged. "I don't know that the prosecutor will buy it any more than you. Jacob says they were outside and she ended up in the bedroom upstairs."

"I've read about head injuries where the person gets up, walks away, and dies later. Is that possible with Justine?"

He shrugged. "The coroner will have to determine that."

"Well, at least we know who killed her, right?"

"Right now, we have him on assault. That's actually all he admitted to."

Brett leaned forward. "What about Lacie?"

"He was still ranting that she was at fault. Right now, she's our guest as well. I was too exhausted to deal with her." He cleared his throat. "Um. Sheridan, I was wondering if you'd be willing to sit in on that interview?"

I could hardly refuse. It was hard enough not to show my excitement while Brett groaned.

CHAPTER 29

When the alarm went off and I had to get up, eat, and get dressed earlier than I wanted, I had second thoughts. Chief Peabody decided we'd start at nine o'clock. Groaning, I was dressed by the time Maddie and Brett left. Not my usual routine though that would have to change by next week and the start of classes.

Preston nodded when I walked in.

"Good morning, Dr. Hendley. I'll let the chief know you're here."

Seated on the bench in the reception area, I didn't have to wait long. The chief stuck his head out and waved me in.

"Morning. Come on back. She's already in the interview room. Coffee?"

"Of course."

We stopped at the break room and grabbed coffees for all of us. We walked into the room and Lacie glared at me.

"Coffee. I asked Sheridan to be here given that you've been my employee for several years now. At every turn, more information points to you being involved. You understand that, don't you?"

She nodded and wrung her hands.

"Let's get this over with. Jacob indicated you were the housekeeper for his parents."

"Yes, sir. For many years, I went over there weekly and helped Justine, until Herman retired. He decided they didn't need as much help with him at home, too. After that it was only once a month. Or if Herman went somewhere and Justine wanted help while he was gone."

He shuffled some papers and handed her telephone records dating back two years ago. "This here shows a call from the Stoneham's land line to your number here at the station, not once, but several times, over two days. What was that all about?"

"Justine wasn't calling to report a crime. She called because Herman died. They were watching television and he slumped over, dead."

"Most people would call for paramedics. Did she want you to call them?"

"No. She was frantic, sure Jacob would sell the house out from under her. She was hysterical, but there was no doubt he was dead."

"So what did you do?"

Lacie shrugged.

The chief exhaled. "Lacie, who helped Justine dress Herman and move him to the backyard and bury him?"

"I did. She was sure she'd be homeless if Jacob found out. We... we cleaned him up and put him in his suit first. She said a prayer over the grave."

"I see. And did you keep helping Justine with housekeeping?"

"Only once in a while. Not often. Not in the last year."

He pulled another page out of his file. I recognized my notes. "The dogs. What can you tell us about the dogs?"

"After Herman died, Justine kept calling – not for help. She was lonely. I suggested she get a dog. She'd always wanted a dog. She didn't want to get one from Mrs. C. There was too much bad history with the Buchanan family and Clover Hill. I searched the internet and gave her information on dogs available and helped her get Rosie."

Her eyes teared up. "I helped Justine call and order dog food and such over the phone. She'd go to Oak Grove to get groceries but there's no pet store there and the grocer didn't have much. Other than church, she and Herman avoided Clover Hill. A couple of weeks later, she told me she didn't need my help as much now that it would just be her in the house and Rosie for company." Lacie shrugged.

The chief pulled another page out and turned it so Lacie could see it. "This shows a call from her to you, again here at the station, two days before Justine was found."

"She called me. She didn't make a lot of sense. She was crying and said she needed my help. Something about a dog, but her speech was hard to understand. I chalked it up to a bad connection and told her I'd come by as soon as I could. That was Sunday, the day Preston called in sick and I worked a double. I didn't get there until the next day after my shift." She wrung her hands and her lips trembled.

"What did you find when you arrived?"

"Dogs. And more dogs. And one of them had a broken leg. I yelled for Justine. She didn't answer. I went inside and … I can't even describe it. I almost got sick. I yelled for her again and searched the house. She was dead – cold dead."

"You didn't think to report it?"

"There was nothing I could do for her. I focused on the dogs. I put the injured dog in my car. I drove my car past Blake Buchanan's property and called for Bridgit and Butch until one came. It was Bridgit. I took her back to the house and showed her the puppies and dogs under the deck. Then I left and watched from the woods as Bridgit picked up a puppy and brought it to the Buchanan property."

She sipped her coffee. "After I knew Blake had the puppy and saw him drive out to the Stoneham's after Bridgit, I knew it was only a matter of time. I took the injured dog to my place and splinted his leg, fed him, and took care of him. I found some others the next day. I later snuck them into the garage at Mrs. C.'s so they could get more care."

I gasped. No wonder Luke thought he was going crazy.

"Where did you find the others?"

"There's a dirt road at the rear of the property. I knew Blake's dogs hadn't gotten that far yet, so I drove there to check it out and found them."

"What can you tell us about Jacob and Helen?"

She snorted. "Jacob? He's a piece of work. Sad excuse of a man. He scared Justine and Helen. Only because he was bigger, Herman stood up to him."

"Anything else?"

She shook her head. I turned to the chief.

"Can I ask her a question?" He nodded.

"Lacie, did you write MYOB on my windshield and send a letter to my home? Slash my tire?"

She glared at me. "You just couldn't let me alone and Mrs. C.? She prodded you. I left the message and sent the letter, yes. Lot of good it did. I didn't slash your tire though."

The chief looked at me and I nodded.

"I think that's all Lacie. You can go home."

She stood up, glared at me, and then left.

"Chief, why isn't she under arrest?"

"Technically, I have no proof she committed a crime. Even the message on your car or the letter didn't include a threat or involve damage."

"Nonetheless, she knew about two deaths and didn't report either of them."

"It will be up to the prosecutor to decide if he wants to pursue it. There's no indication she or Justine were disrespectful in burying Herman. No indication she contributed to the death. The legal glitch there is that Justine didn't notify social security or the retirement agency – she collected money fraudulently."

He grimaced. "But there's no indication Lacie benefited from that. She still may be charged in relation to the fraud. She didn't admit to any consideration of social security or retirement monies though, only Jacob selling the house. And Lacie didn't benefit from Justine's death."

"Huh?"

"There are loopholes in the laws regarding reporting a death. I looked it up and as long as they didn't do something ... something gruesome or disrespectful to the body, and the death didn't result from a crime, there isn't an actual law that says a person has to report a death. I'll give this information to the prosecutor's office and they'll decide how to handle it."

I nodded and stood up to leave. "What about he was buried in the backyard?"

"If it had been in Clover Hill, that would be against the zoning laws for sure. In another area, they would have to, at least note, the location of the burial on a map with the property clerk. It would depend on the jurisdiction and the applicable laws. Again, the prosecutor will have to sort through all the legal documents to determine what laws apply to that property to determine if that was a crime."

He paused and then continued. "Bottom line, even with the fraud, Lacie didn't incriminate herself. Thank you for sitting in. I wasn't quite sure what to expect from her. Anything stand out to you?"

"The timeline. I noticed the date of Justine's call. Wasn't that the day Jacob said he was there?"

"That's correct."

"If that call was after Jacob was there, that means she regained consciousness, at least long enough to make the call and go upstairs to lie down."

He nodded. "We'll never know if Justine was calling about herself, the injured dog, or both. Or if it would have made a difference if he'd called for help for her or if Lacie had."

CHAPTER 30

We'd invited Angie, Alex and Karla over for dinner. Maddie needed an audience and help deciding on which of four songs to use for the audition.

Although the weather was a bit chilly, Brett decided to grill some steaks, mostly watching the grill from inside.

"Did they ever find homes for all those dogs?" Karla asked.

Maddie immediately replied, "Almost, but there are still some puppies left, and the mamas. Do you know anyone looking for a dog?"

We adults all laughed.

"You did a great job of setting the table. Why don't you kids go watch television until everything's ready?"

With that suggestion, they quickly disappeared, Maddie still talking about the dogs who needed homes. Brett smiled with obvious fatherly pride as he watched them leave. Then he turned to Angie and me.

"Wine, Angie? Sher and I often have a glass with dinner. Afraid we don't have a lot of choices, mostly whites."

She nodded and added, "White is fine. Is the murder solved?"

I groaned and Brett shrugged.

"The legal system isn't always simple. The son – Jacob – is being held for involuntary manslaughter, assault, and several other violations, including slashing Sheridan's tire. Enough to keep him as guest of the district and the county. Now the attorneys will pull together all the evidence and decide which ones they will move forward with, given all available evidence."

"A son killing his own mother." Angie shook her head. After a second's hesitation, she asked, "What about Luke?"

I laughed. "Certainly a surprising change in attitude toward adults and compassion in six months' time. His ability – and willingness – to step up in a crisis was impressive. Hopefully, with continued support from his parents and Blake, he'll turn out okay."

"His uncle's behavior landed him in prison. That may have set a lot of changes into place with him, his parents, and Blake. That said, I still don't want my daughter spending too much time around him unchaperoned."

"Oh, Brett, I suspect you're going to feel that way about most boys by the time Maddie's fourteen. Even my Alex. It's only natural. Hard to have daughters and hope everyone's brought their sons up right. After her skating experience, Karla fancies she's in love with Dan. I'm sure that will fade as she meets other boys, but it is always a concern with daughters."

"It's not too late to teach her some self-defense is it?"

We all laughed as the timer dinged and he bolted outside to check the steaks. Dinner was lively and switched from dogs and murder to auditions.

It was a simple meal with lots of laughter. Then audition time. What I didn't realize was that Alex also was auditioning. He sang for us as well. A little biased, we all concluded they'd both get in. No surprise, we all preferred the songs from musicals.

***

What with everything going on, it was Thursday before I thought to call Helen and see what was happening. We met at the local coffee shop.

"Hi. How are you doing, Helen?"

"Good. Better. I'm not really sure."

I chuckled. "A lot has happened very quickly."

"Yes, and I'm working on getting as much settled as I can. I've talked to my daughter or son every day with updates. The memorial for my mother will be tomorrow. Just a quiet ceremony with Pastor Pete."

I nodded. At least she'd have closure on both deaths. "Do you know what is going to happen with Jacob?"

"Yes. And no." She shook her head and took a sip of her coffee. "His attorney is trying to work out a plea bargain. I don't understand that whole process. And I talked to his wife. His drinking and gambling. She served him with divorce papers the week he came here. His behavior took a toll at work as well. He lost his job the same week."

I waited and she continued. "I took your advice and contacted the estate attorney my son found. And you were correct. At the bank, with my signature on everything? I am the owner. Only all the accounts are frozen. Social security and the retirement program have to determine the difference between what has been paid and what my mother would have gotten if they had been informed when my father had died. Then penalties may apply. And they may be charging Lacie with fraud."

She shrugged. "It's all up in the air. I'll have to come back for both if they go to trial."

She took a deep breath. "Hopefully, there's enough money in the accounts to cover the penalties and my attorney's fees. As far as I can tell, my parents lived very frugally and there should be."

I cringed. Hopefully, she wouldn't end up owing money on top of everything else. "What about the house?"

"My attorney's sure that with the charges against him, Jacob will not be able to inherit anything, even with a plea bargain. Everything will go to probate. And likely to me."

"Assuming you do inherit the house and property, what will you do?"

"I've been back there the last two days and almost all the boxes and junk are gone. I went to the food bank and paid some people to help. Lacie came by too. Looks more like I remember it."

She glanced away and then continued. "Still, no way I'd want to live there, nor is it being sold to JJ Properties. With all that's happened, until the estate is sorted out, I can't really do anything with the house or property anyway. For now, the house is being closed up. That's been agreed to by the law firm my father used and my attorney."

"That makes sense." I nodded again. "When will you return to Seattle?"

"Tomorrow after the memorial. Honestly, Sheridan? It's all too much for me to handle. I'm still in shock. My parents. Jacob. Legal issues. Money issues. I need to sit down and figure it all out."

We enjoyed our coffee and pastry. I gave her a hug, wishing her well. And I gave her my phone number in case she wanted to talk. Then I went to Pets and Paws.

Flurries hit my windshield and I smiled. Just a fleeting reminder it was winter. I parked my car and couldn't help but glance toward the garage. The door was closed tight. Once inside the house, I could hear Mrs. Chantilly humming a tune in the kitchen.

"Hi, Mrs. Chantilly. How's everything going?" I stashed my purse and jacket in the cabinet.

"The biscuits are almost ready. I don't know what Lacie's going to do now. She's been suspended. Blake thought I'd move into Justine's house. Not likely. This was my grandmother's house, you know. She had a lot of dogs here. I cleaned it all up. I hope you and Maddie continue to help out. She has a lovely voice."

"We'll still be helping out on the weekend. I'll resume my usual afternoon schedule on Tuesday and Thursday. Have you scheduled an adoption day?"

"What a great idea. I'll have to see when Luke is going to be available. Horatio still needs some time and Ghost, too. I don't know why Luke named him that. He's very real and not even gray. The puppies. Vanna took pictures and she's working on finding them homes. Susie will be in later."

"Good. I can send some pics of the puppies out to the rescues to share as well. For now, I'll start in the back then. I'll probably have to wait for Luke to take Horatio out. I think I can handle Ghost."

"I'll bring the biscuits when they're ready."

I checked crates and was happy to see most of the dogs were looking happy and healthy. Even Horatio and Ghost. Mrs. Chantilly came in with biscuits and they all enjoyed their treats. I'd finished with all the others and was helping Ghost stand up when Luke walked in.

"Hold up, Dr. H. I'll take him out."

"Okay. Everyone else except this one and Horatio have been out. With the casts, I'm not quite sure…"

He smiled. "Easiest is to pick him up." He undid the top of the crate, reached in and picked him up.

"Good thinking. I'll clean out the crate while you take him out and then we can take care of Horatio."

Mission accomplished, I collected my belongings as Susie came in. I checked on the puppies to give Maddie an update and then I went home with hopes that life would return to normal. Or at least as normal as can be with a detective husband, a teenager, and two dogs.

ABOUT THE AUTHOR

I hope you enjoyed this cozy mystery about dog rescues and community members chipping in when needed. Please support mental health efforts, as well as animal shelters and rescues in your community. If you or someone you know needs mental health assistance, please seek help.

About Christa Nardi

Christa Nardi (pen name) is an accomplished writer and an avid reader. Her love of mysteries began with Nancy Drew and other teen mysteries, as well as Perry Mason and similar detective series on television. Her favorite authors have shifted from Carolyn Keene and Earl Stanley Gardner to more contemporary mystery and crime authors over time.

Christa has authored the 5-book Cold Creek cozy mystery series with the new spinoff series featuring the protagonist, Sheridan Hendley, a professor and psychologist. She also authors a third mystery series, the Stacie Maroni series. She co-authors the Hannah and Tamar Mystery series for teens and young adults with Cassidy Salem. When not reading or writing, Christa enjoys travel with her husband, and playing with three dogs and three grand-daughters.

You can find Christa Nardi on Amazon, Goodreads, Bookbub, Facebook, and Twitter
- Email: cccnardi@gmail.com

- Blog: Christa Reads and Writes
  (https://www.christanardi.blogspot.com) for
  spotlights and reviews – mostly mystery, but
  occasionally a romance slips in.
- Sign up for the monthly newsletter with
  updates and sale/new release announcements
  and giveaways
  http://smarturl.it/NardiNewsletter

Series by Christa Nardi

Cold Creek Series featuring Sheridan Hendley

- *Murder at Cold Creek College (Cold Creek #1)*
- *Murder in the Arboretum (Cold Creek #2)*
- *Murder at the Grill (Cold Creek #3)*
- *Murder in the Theater (Cold Creek #4)*
- *A Murder and a Wedding (Cold Creek #5)*

Sheridan Hendley Mystery Series

- *A New Place, Another Murder (Sheridan Hendley #1)*
- *Dogs and More Dogs, Another Murder (Sheridan Hendley #2)*

Stacie Maroni Mystery Series

- *Prestige, Privilege and Murder (A Stacie Maroni #1)*
- *Foundations, Funny Business and Murder (A Stacie Maroni Mystery #2)*
- *Deceptions, Denial and Murder (A Stacie Maroni Mystery #3)*

Teen/Young Adult Mystery Series with Cassidy Salem – The Hannah and Tamar Mystery Series

- *The Mysterious Package*
- *Mrs. Tedesco's Missing Cookbook*
- *The Misplaced Dog*
- *Malicious Mischief*

New to Sheridan Hendley, read on for the back story and her debut series at Cold Creek.

INTRODUCTION TO THE COLD CREEK SERIES AND SHERIDAN HENDLEY

Cold Creek, VA is a fictitious, small town of about 3000 residents (not including the student population) closest to and East of Roanoke and South of Lynchburg. Cold Creek College (also fictitious) was initially a boarding school and catered to the wealthier families. Cold Creek came into existence to support the school. Over time the school morphed into a private four-year college of about 1500 students. As the school expanded, so did the community. More detailed history is provided in the first book in the series, MURDER AT COLD CREEK COLLEGE...

The series' protagonist is Sheridan Hendley, a professor and psychologist in the Psychology Department. Bright and curious, she is a natural amateur sleuth. Moreover, she is an advocate for the underdog, or in this series, the obvious suspect. Intended as a cozy mystery series, each book is a mystery that is completed within that book - a stand-alone mystery. Relationships and romance, however, continue to evolve with each new book.

MURDER AT COLD CREEK COLLEGE is the first in the series. A dead body is not a good way to start the fall semester for anyone, but especially the victim. Adam Millberg is a womanizer and the suspect list is long. Is infidelity the only motive? Sexual harassment? Sheridan is motivated to prove her best friend's innocence and help the nice looking detective.

"It was a fun romp, well-paced and suspenseful, with just the right amount of humor, romance and intrigue thrown in."

"The story was well-plotted and the twists and turns the story takes make it a very enjoyable read."

In the second in the series, **MURDER IN THE ARBORETUM,** *there is no obvious motive, no obvious reason for Justin Blake to be in the Arboretum. Many question the guilt of the convenient scapegoat and Sheridan works hard to prove his innocence. Tensions are high and Sheridan's sleuthing is more dangerous. Is it time for those self-defense classes or too late?*

"The story line was not predicable, taking a few unexpected turns as the mystery unfolded."

"I just couldn't put this one down. I was hooked from the first chapter."

In **MURDER AT THE GRILL,** *Sheridan once again finds herself trying to prove someone is innocent. This time it's her favorite waitress at the family owned restaurant. As Sheridan works to unravel the family secrets, the family closes ranks. Not easily stopped, Sheridan finds herself in dangerous situations.*

"Enjoyable mystery that makes sense."

"The characters are complex, the plots hold my interest, and the writing style is enjoyable."

"Readers of both cozy mysteries and romantic suspense will find MURDER AT THE GRILL very appealing."

In book *4, MURDER IN THE THEATER: It'd be the season to be jolly if only someone hadn't set the stage for murder. When a student is arrested for the crime, Professor Sheridan Hendley is cast in the role of amateur sleuth. Tensions run high, friendships are strained, and the college administration is beginning to panic. As the plot thickens Sheridan is yet again drawn deeper into danger. Will she find the truth before the final curtain call?*

"This series is a solid murder mystery series, however, the gentle romances that have bloomed within its tales are enjoyable and equally attractive to the cozy genre reader."

"Finding the murderer of a man reviled by all may be one tough assignment and Marty is too close to the case to be much help. The investigation competes with family stress as Thanksgiving nears. I love that Sheridan's personal life as well as her job flow through the investigation helping to maintain a balance for the reader and greater insight into our protagonist."

Book 5, A MURDER AND A WEDDING, is the last in the series. Solving a murder wasn't on the wedding planner's checklist. With so many changes in her life, sleuthing is the last thing on the mind of Cold Creek College's amateur sleuth. That is until the victim is the manager of the perfect wedding venue. When Sheridan visits Hidden Oaks, she senses there is more underfoot than meets the eye. Can she put the pieces together and have her wedding, too?

"Easy read with not a too complicated plot, but just enough to keep you interested. Also a bit of romance…"

"I really enjoyed Murder and a Wedding. … Lots of plot twists as our professor prepares to leave her college and move to a new town with her soon to be husband. Very entertaining."

A NEW PLACE, ANOTHER MURDER
A Sheridan Hendley Mystery #1

And the first in the "spin-off" series to start the Sheridan Hendley series:

Sometimes you need to be careful what you wish for.

Pretty much settled into her new home in Appomattox with Brett and his daughter, Sheridan longs for something to keep her busy. That is, until Maddie and her new friend are framed for theft and murder. Not quite the distraction she had hoped for, but she'll turn over every rock to prove their innocence. In the process, she learns about the powerful Buchanan family and the history of the local community. Will the truth come out before the person calling the shots takes Sheridan and Maddie out of the picture?

"Nardi brought along the characters I loved from Cold Creek (Sheridan, Brett, Maddie, and Charlie, Sheridan's Sheltie) put them in new situations, bring new life to the characters. I also liked that Sheridan keeps in contact with former colleagues at Cold Creek College. This made Sheridan seem even more real to me."

"A very down to earth read. A normal family that finds itself embroiled in murder and crime due to his job as detective and hers as nosy Nellie. Great characters that you could meet anywhere."

Stay tuned … the third in the series will be out later in 2019!

Made in the USA
Monee, IL
15 October 2020